THE BOY NEXT DOOR

A SMALL TOWN ROMANCE

Hazel Kelly is the author of several romance novels.
She was born in the United States and lives in Ireland.

ALSO BY HAZEL KELLY

The Tempted Series

The Fated Series

The Club Abbott Series

The Wanted Series

The Craved Series

The Devoured Series

The Exposed Series

Available from Amazon.com & Amazon.co.uk.
Also available on Kindle and other devices.

THE BOY NEXT DOOR

A SMALL TOWN ROMANCE

Hazel Kelly

First published 2016.

ISBN-13: 978-1539605478

Printed and bound by CreateSpace.

Cover Artwork – © 2016 L.J. Anderson of Mayhem Cover Creations

"The best gift in life is a second chance."

Prologue

He was the one that got away, and I knew it before I ever broke things off with him.

I didn't want to end it, but at the time I believed it was the right thing to do... Because of who he was, who he wanted to become, and because of where I came from.

I loved him more than I loved anything, but I thought he could do better.

Even then I knew I'd never be able to replicate the happiness I found with him, in him.

I tried, of course, but based on my experience, I've come to believe there really is one right person for everyone.

And not only did I let my soulmate get away, I pushed him as far as he would go.

As a result, I was convinced I deserved every second of loneliness the universe handed me.

After all, I'd shunned the greatest gift it could offer anyone: True Love.

But luckily for me, it turns out the universe is just as stubborn as I am.

ONE

- Laney -

When I found the ring, I knew I couldn't marry him.

Not that it wasn't beautiful.

It was. In fact, it was princess cut perfection, and I was tempted to slip it on my finger.

Just to see how it would look.

After all, what would be the harm? I knew it was meant for me.

But at the same time, it wasn't. It was meant for the woman Henry thought I wanted to be, the women he thought I was. And that wasn't me at all.

It was all my fault, of course, for leading him on. And obviously I'd lead him too far if he believed I was ready for an engagement ring. But I didn't mean to mislead him.

Like I said, it was only when I found the ring that I realized I didn't love him enough. Not like that. Not like you're supposed to love someone when you say yes to loving them through sickness and health and all those other extremes that represent the crapshoot of goodies life might offer.

I'd been in love before and this wasn't it. I could feel it in my bones as I tilted the box in my hands, watching the sunbeams bounce off the color trapped inside the diamond.

I wanted to love Henry that way. I'd spent the last year and a half convincing myself that that head over heels feeling was right around the corner, but finding the ring was proof that it wasn't.

I felt nothing. Nothing but disappointment in myself.

Why couldn't I love him back the way he was obviously prepared to love me?

He was an amazing catch and a great provider. And not once had he ever made me feel small because he was a successful accountant who was actually important enough that had to keep his shoes shined, and I was a retired wannabe artist who pretended to be a waitress every day in hideous, practical sneakers that usually floated on a thin layer of crushed hash brown mixed with lemon cleaner and a slippery coating of grease.

When I saw the ring, I should've started doing fucking cartwheels and crying and ovulating like a normal woman.

Instead, I was looking back and forth between the ring and his sock drawer, wondering if I could just put the box back where I found it and pretend I'd never seen it.

But what then?

There were no good choices.

I could wait for him to pop the question, then let him down easy and hope he'd be understanding.

But I knew from experience the only time that ever worked out was on the Bachelorette, and it wasn't because the potential suitors were better behaved than regular guys. It was because there were cameras everywhere.

I suppose I could slip into conversation how I really wasn't ready to get married and hope he'd take the hint.

But then what? Just keep going through the motions as if I still believed we might have a bright future together?

Maybe I could turn into some kind of unbearable monster overnight that no one in their right mind would ever possibly commit to.

Granted, that was by far the most fun sounding option. The most cinematic.

I could start using his toothbrush, burping in his face, and breaking things. I could decorate his apartment in bright pinks and leave crazy books around like *Why He Doesn't Really Need Space* and *Why Real Men Love Bitches*.

My cooking was already below average, but I could start saying nasty things about little kids on TV- maybe even tell him what I really thought of his relationship with his mother or let it slip that I've always wondered if his dad was well hung.

Ugh. Okay. So I wouldn't go quite that far.

And to be honest, I wasn't capable of doing any of that. Not to Henry, anyway. He was too good. He didn't deserve it.

Plus, after touching other people's dirty plates all day and pretending that I thought it was cute that they let their toddler pour his own syrup or make her own powdered sugar finger paintings on the table, I really didn't have the energy to stage such a catastrophic mess on my own turf.

Not that it mattered.

Because I already knew what I was going to do. I was going to flee. It was the only option.

I couldn't possibly look him in the eye over dinner later and pretend I hadn't found it. I couldn't tip toe around believing he might jump around the corner and drop to his knee any second.

After all, I knew what it was like to break someone's heart, and it was the last thing I ever wanted to do the first time I did it.

So I sure as hell wasn't going to sit by and do nothing if I thought I might have to do it again.

I needed time. And I needed to put the ring down before I got my fingerprints all over the little velvet box.

I took one last look at it. It made me sick to think how different the face I was making was from the one he probably made when he was picking it out.

Then I closed the box gently so it wouldn't make a sound (as if he might hear it in his office on the other side of New York) and returned it to the back of the drawer where he kept his collection of black work socks twisted into careful little balls.

Seriously, even his sock drawer was proof that I didn't deserve him.

I mean, I was only in this mess because I'd failed to keep up with my laundry like other adults seemed to do so effortlessly. And I still might've avoided this problem if I'd happily slapped on a pair of dirty socks. But nooo, I wanted to be fresh footed on a Monday like some kind of princess.

I groaned.

If only I had someone to call.

Unfortunately, all my friends in this city were Henry's friends, too. Except for my friends at work, and I couldn't vent to them because I had to give them an excuse for why I couldn't be there for a few days.

Because I desperately needed some fresh air.

And to be on the safe side, I figured I could do with more fresh air than fit in Central Park. Plus, a safe distance would help make sure Henry couldn't pop in while I was hatching a plan to free him from my broken, inadequate love.

Fortunately, I'd only moved in three months ago so it didn't take long to chuck some stuff in a bag. Not that I had much anyway.

My former apartment was only about twice the size of a standard parking space. It also featured the occasional six legged hissing guest and an elevator straight out of a Hitchcock film.

Needless to say, the conversation about who should be the one to move when we opted to cohabitate was a relatively short one.

And it had been a wonderful few months, some of the best I'd had in my adult life quite frankly.

And he had to go and ruin it by buying a damn ring.

TWO

- Connor -

I faked to the left before dribbling around Dave and landing another layup.

"Is it me or are you getting rusty?" I asked, grabbing the ball and jogging back towards center court.

He bent over and set his hands on his knees. "I think it's that you're getting taller."

I laughed and held the ball against my hip. "Something tells me that's not it."

He leaned up and wiped the sweat off his brow. "Would it be really pussy of me to blame the kid?"

I narrowed my eyes. "How old is she now?"

"A year," he said. "And the other two are vampires."

I laughed. "I thought vampires were superfast."

He walked to the side of the crumbling court and grabbed his water bottle off the bench. "They get it from their mother's side."

"I suppose it's not a bad excuse," I said. "I did notice a few grays the other day."

"Fuck you," he said, water dribbling down his chin. "You did not."

"Maybe I imagined it," I said, shooting a free throw from the line. It swooshed in, nothing but net, and I ran to collect it.

"I'm not even twenty eight," Dave said, sitting on the bench.

"Didn't your dad go gray prematurely?" I asked, walking back to the line.

"Didn't your dad teach you some manners?"

I shot again and watched the ball hit the backboard and go in.

"And don't guy's hair genes come from their mom's side?"

"Good point," I said, walking over to him. "In which case there's definitely no hope for you."

He glared at me. "Someday your kids are going to make your thick blond waves fall out, too. Then we'll see who's gloating."

"I'm not gloating. I'm just saying you seem a bit rusty."

"Maybe you just aren't rusting fast enough," he said. "Maybe you should come on patrol with me later and see what breaking up gangland warfare does for your stress levels?"

I sat on the bench next to him and wiped some sweat on my shoulder. "Gangs in Glastonbury, huh? Would that be the gang that sells the lemonade on Fourth Street or the gang that washes cars and sells Thin Mints on Tenth?"

"So there are no gangs." He leaned back. "You got me."

I slammed some water, which was grossly warm from sitting in the sun.

"Sometimes I wish we'd see some more action around here to be honest," he said. "The biggest problem we had last year was when we thought Mrs. Johnson's purse had been stolen."

"Didn't she just leave it at the fabric store?"

He nodded.

"At least no one can accuse you of not doing your job."

"True," he said. "What about you? Haven't seen many sick animals around so you must be doing well."

"Busier than ever," I said. "And people have started coming from out of state to see me because of my new invention."

"That rubber wine stopper you showed me?"

I rolled my eyes. "It's not a wine stopper. It's an artificial animal foot."

"Right."

"I know it's hard for you to get excited about it, but if your dog lost her leg for some reason, you'd be panicking in my office and begging me to bring back the pep in her step, too."

"So it works?"

I nodded. "Over ninety percent of the time."

"Cool."

I hung an arm over the back of the bench. "It'll be even cooler if the patent comes through."

"Because you'll get paid every time another vet wants to be a hero?"

"Pretty much."

"When will you know?"

I shrugged. "There's no telling with these things. It's all paperwork and paper pushing and waiting around for papers to be processed."

"Well, I'll keep my fingers crossed for you- and not just because we don't know who's going to be this year's local hero in the Fourth of July parade."

"I'm not doing that regardless."

He dropped his chin and raised his eyebrows. "If I ask you to wear a flag and throw candy in my parade, you'll fucking do it."

I groaned. "That is so not why I moved back here. And it's not your parade just because the mayor thinks you have a nice speaking voice."

"Everyone thinks I have a nice speaking voice."

"Whatever, the local hero should be some retiree who's running out of chances to be the local hero."

"Hey," he said, raising his hands. "I'm open to suggestions."

"How about Billy Porter?"

Dave furrowed his brow. "Hardware store Billy Porter?"

"Yeah, why not? He's never been properly recognized for setting up that sump pump hotline a decade ago, which has kept countless basements in this town from flooding. Plus, he didn't charge anyone for borrowing his extra snowplows last winter when the blizzard rolled in. The guy's a saint."

"You've sold me," Dave said. "I'll run it by the mayor."

"Maybe you could get one of the local gangs to make a giant sump pump for the top of the float?"

He shook his head. "You're an idiot."

"Are you kidding? A giant red, white, and blue sump pump?! Who wouldn't be pumped to see that?"

"You're so right," he said. "What a treat that would be for everyone."

I smiled and tilted my face up towards the late afternoon sun. "Any other problems you need solved now that you have my full attention?"

"My girls want a treehouse."

"You're on your own there," I said. "Why don't you get them one for the ground like a normal parent? They make pink ones and everything."

"They already have one of those."

"Maybe one of the local gangs could conveniently steal it for a few days," I said. "Then you can be the hero that brings it back right after they're all cried out over thinking they'll never see it again."

"I love that idea," he said. "But I'm not sure Amber would be up for it."

"Do you have to run everything by her?"

He tilted his head. "Do you know nothing about marriage?"

"Can't say I do."

"Speaking of which, I meant to ask if you'd come by ours this weekend. We're barbequing for some family reason I can't remember. Probably the anniversary of someone's first bite of solid food or some other bullshit. Should be fun."

"Is this your way of tricking me into mingling with the single ladies of Glastonbury?"

He shrugged. "It's not really a trick if you know about it."

"True."

"Plus, it will be more fun for me if you're there. Amber's lined up a babysitter so she's guaranteed to hit the white wine until it hits her back. And I could use a trusted grill master in case I have to piss."

"Won't all your work buddies be there?"

"Some of them," he said. "But I only invited them to make you look good."

"Oh look," I whispered, nodding over his shoulder "Here comes one of those gangs you warned me about."

Dave turned around just as some teenagers approached the court.

"You guys using the court or can we shoot some hoops?" the one in the Jordan's said.

I leaned forward. "It's all yours."

"But play on this side to be safe, guys," Dave added. "The pavement on that side's a disgrace."

"We know," the boy said. "Thanks." Then he turned and threw the ball to a friend before dropping his Gatorade, pulling up his sagging pants, and strutting onto the court.

"How long has the court been busted up like this?" I asked.

Dave scanned the faded grey pavement. "It started crumbling during the recession, and it's only gotten worse."

"Someone should really fix that," I said.

"Yeah," Dave said. "Someone should."

THREE

- Laney -

It only took me a few hours on the interstate to get to Glastonbury, and as soon as I turned onto the off ramp, I felt like I could breathe again.

At the light, I tried to ignore my left ring finger, which seemed to almost be taunting me with the fact that it wanted something different. But its silent jeers weren't enough to make the rest of my body feel guilty.

However, I did feel a little bad about blowing off work, and my boss hadn't exactly been gracious about it. But I always took the shittiest shifts and that was- fingers crossed- my job security taken care of.

As I cruised through the city center, I couldn't help but feel uplifted by all the friendly faces and the quaint vibe of the colorful town. If New York was an over the top triple fudge Sunday, Glastonbury was an unassuming Nilla Wafer.

Sure, some people are all about the big and decadent, and I'd been trying to become one of those people for years. Unfortunately, I was always in the mood for a Nilla Wafer, and that was the point of difference on which the Big Apple just couldn't compete.

The cities were like night and day, and the evidence was everywhere.

While waiting at a crosswalk, the family crossing the street smiled at me. All of them. It was evident that the mom had made clear the lesson that you always make eye contact with the driver so you can get safely across.

In New York, the rule was to always keep at least one person between you and the closest bumper.

A few minutes later, I saw I woman drop a piece of paper, and two people took off after it to help her steal it back from the wind.

In the city, you had to hold onto your possessions so tightly the wind would never get ahold of anything in the first place. And if it did, you better hope it wasn't important because your shit was as good as gone.

Five minutes later, feeling no less panicked than when I found the ring but breathing much better, I pulled my little two door Chevy into my Grandma Helly's driveway.

Her house hadn't changed much since I'd first come to live with her when I was thirteen. Except for the flag by the front door, which she changed every month into whatever the brightest seasonal eyesore she could find was.

At the minute, a jumbo duckling waved in the breeze, providing such a bright flash of yellow it was surprising the sun even bothered showing up.

On my way to the door, I felt a pang of guilt that I hadn't been up in a year, but hopefully my negligence would be forgiven in light of my surprise visit.

I knocked and rang the bell, but there was no answer so I walked around to the back door.

The scene I found made my heart grow two sizes.

Grandma Helly was in her gardening knee pads in front of an upturned Frisbee full of fresh milk. In front of her, three cats were lapping away while she blabbed to them like they were there not for the milk, but for an audience with her.

"I hope I'm not interrupting," I said, stepping onto one of the irregularly shaped stones that formed a giant Celtic pattern on the ground in the back garden.

Her face lit up when she saw me. "Laney!" She rose to her feet like a woman half her age. "What a nice surprise."

We met halfway across the slate stones, and she gave me a smothery grandma hug that was strangely grounding. Then she leaned back and admired my face like it was the ceiling of the Sistine Chapel and she'd waited her whole life to behold it.

"Glad to see you, too, Grandma," I said. "I hope you're not too busy for another thirsty visitor."

"Not at all, and don't mind them," she said, waving a hand towards her furry guests. "You know me. I don't even like cats. Let's get a cool drink, and you can tell me everything."

I smiled. She was always insisting people tell her *everything* even if there was nothing going on. I'd forgotten how much pressure it could be to keep her entertained. Not that she wasn't always ready to jump in with a story of her own, many of which complete fabrications.

"There's not much to tell," I lied, unsure of whether I was ready to discuss that morning's incident out loud.

"Don't give me that bull," she said, holding the screen door open for me. "You didn't come all this way because you've got nothing to talk about."

I walked through the mudroom into the kitchen. "I see you're still into crystals."

"Crystals are into me," she said, opening the fridge door. "Now for what we're going to get into you."

"Water's fine."

"Nonsense," she said. "I just made lemonade this morning."

"Perfect."

"Are you hungry?" she asked, setting a frosty looking pitcher on the counter.

My eyes bounced around the flat crystals that hung in front of the kitchen window like stained glass. "Is that pink one new? It's pretty."

She furrowed her thin brows. "You're attracted to the pink one?"

I shrugged. "Yeah."

She took a deep breath and pulled two tall glasses down from the cupboard. "You want to tell me what's on your mind?"

"Not food," I said. "To answer your question."

"Are you sure?" she asked, pouring two glasses. "I won't even make you clear your own dirty plate. As a special treat."

I laughed. "That's very thoughtful of you, but I'm fine for the minute."

"Suit yourself," she said, shaking her head and setting the glasses down on the stone coasters I'd unstacked.

"I'll let you know if I need something."

"Please do," she said. "You deserve a bit of pampering. I know how hard you work in that diner."

"If only I had more to show for it."

"Is that what this is about?" she asked. "Are things bad at work?"

"Not any more than usual."

"Is it your boyfriend? Have you guys had a disagreement?"

"No." I scrunched my face. "But I kind of drove here to prevent one."

She clasped her hands in her lap. "Tell me everything."

"I'd rather talk about how great the garden is coming along first."

"The garden isn't going anywhere," she said, leaning back in her chair.

"Or get filled in on the Glastonbury gossip I've missed out on since my last visit."

"You'll enjoy that more after dinner when I've got a drink in my hand. Besides, you know I think gossiping during daylight hours is tacky."

I took a deep breath and looked in her kind eyes. "The truth is, Grandma, I don't want to burden you."

She threw her eyes to the sky and then leaned forward, placing one of her soft hands on mine. "Honey, I've lived thirty five lives in the last four hundred years. I promise I can handle it."

I raised my eyebrows. "Are you sure you want to know?"

"I'm sure," she said, resting her chin on her hands. "Tell me everything."

FOUR

- Connor -

I whistled up the stairs. "Sarge! You coming or staying?"

A moment later, the young golden retriever appeared on the landing.

"Staying?" I asked.

He laid down at the top of the steps.

"I'll take that as a yes," I mumbled, closing the door behind me and picking up the basket of fresh tomatoes I'd left on my front step.

It had been almost a year, and it still felt weird closing the front door of my house without calling good bye to my parents. Fortunately, Sarge had made the place feel a little less empty.

I made my way down the sidewalk and over to the house next door, wondering what compelled Helly to put up those godawful flags.

I liked a bit of color as much as the next guy and animals were my thing, but a giant cartoon duckling waving in the wind was a bit more fun than I needed to have on the average walk to my mailbox. Or her front door.

I knocked and rang the bell, deciding if she wasn't home I'd just leave the basket on her back porch.

But just as I was about to step down from the stoop, the door opened.

My heart stopped when I saw her.

It was all I could do not to drop the tomatoes.

At first, we just stared at each other, me and the girl next door, the girl I'd once wanted everything with, the girl who broke my heart like it was nothing.

We stared at each other like we were kids again and had only just discovered that the opposite sex was interesting.

But neither of us said anything.

It felt like an eternity, even though it was probably only a few seconds.

Then again, that's all it takes for everything to come flooding back, all it takes to irritate the scars of a broken heart.

A few seconds was all it took for her to change my life the first time I saw her, too, and I could almost feel it happening again: the earth shifting below my feet, the clouds parting, the hormonal adolescent confusion setting in.

"Laney," I said. She hadn't changed a bit. Her hair was still the same dirty blonde, her eyes the same pool blue. Even the way her short black t-shirt hung off her breasts was familiar. So much for spending all those years trying to forget what she looked like.

"Connor."

"What are you doing here?" I asked, wondering why I couldn't have come in my uniform or, at the very least, a clean goddamn shirt. What had I done to deserve her catching me in my college sweats with a basket of fucking tomatoes?

I considered backing all the way down the driveway, disappearing around the corner, and letting her think she'd imagined the whole thing. Of course, then I would be far away from her again. And I'd tried that. It was even harder than being near her.

"I was going to ask you the same question."

I raised the basket. "I was just going to drop off some tomatoes for Helly." It sounded even less cool when I said it out loud.

"Tomatoes?" She stared at the basket but didn't reach for it.

I nodded. "They've sort of taken over."

"Taken over what?"

"My backyard."

She squinted at me.

"Or rather, what was formerly my parent's backyard."

She furrowed her brow. "You moved back home?"

"My folks moved to Florida." I couldn't tell if she wasn't happy to see me or if she was just similarly shocked. Not that that made any sense. The odds were good we'd run into each other eventually. But I never thought-

"You look good," she said, her eyes softening.

I did my best not to blatantly check her out. "So do you."

"Do you want to come in?" she asked, stepping back to open the door wider.

"Inside?"

She laughed. "Yeah. For a drink or something?"

Inside? What kind of moron was I? As if she meant back into her heart. Cop on, man. "Sure."

She closed the door behind me, and I set the tomatoes on the bench in the entryway. Then I followed her into the kitchen, the air seeming full of static everywhere we went. Should I have hugged her? She didn't try to hug me. God this was awful.

I couldn't believe Sarge abandoned me at a time like this. It was like that little jerk knew I was walking into something awkward.

"So," she said, pulling two glasses down from the cupboard.

I pulled a chair out from the small round table and sat down. "So?"

"What have you been up to?" She pulled a pitcher out of the fridge and turned her eyes back on me.

I still couldn't tell if I was happy to see her. "Since when?"

"Since I last saw-" She stopped herself. "Since college."

"I went to vet school," I said.

"In Cali?"

I nodded.

She pursed her lips. "Why didn't you stay out there?"

"I like the blondes on the East Coast better."

She cast her eyes down and brought the drinks over.

"Thanks."

"Thank Helly when you see her," she said. "She made it fresh this morning."

"Seriously, though, I missed this side of the country. It's homier here, and I'm not exactly surfer dude material."

"You look the part."

"Don't get me wrong, I learned to surf and everything. I'd just rather snowboard."

"And your folks' house?" she asked.

"I bought it from them when they told me they were moving."

"I thought they liked it here?"

"They did," I said, laying a hand on the table. "But my mom's got Alzheimer's."

"Oh my god, Connor." The color drained from her cheeks. "I'm so sorry."

"I didn't mean to upset you-"

"No, I'm glad you told me."

Frankly, I wasn't sure why I did, but it's hard to keep secrets from someone you used to tell everything to, someone whose own secrets you used to keep. Still kept.

I leaned back in my chair. "My dad wanted to stay here where things were familiar. He thought that might help her hold on a bit longer."

Laney nodded.

"But my mom didn't want to lose it in front of her friends. She said she'd rather lose it in front of people whose opinions didn't matter to her. That and she said if her days were numbered they might as well be sunny."

Laney's glassy eyes smiled. "It was sweet of your dad to do what she wanted."

"I know, especially when he would've had so much more support here. But he could tell she'd made her mind up."

Laney took a sip of lemonade and licked her lips.

My body fired in all the ways it shouldn't have. "On the plus side, she forgot she was a smoker."

She raised her eyebrows. "I didn't even realize that could happen."

"Me neither. But two weeks ago she came across a pack and accused my dad of smoking Slim Cuts behind her back."

"What did he do?" she asked.

"He said he was really sorry and that he didn't know what got into him, and then he threw them away."

"And that was that?"

I nodded.

"Every cloud, huh?"

"Yeah," I said, thinking of the pain in my chest I felt as a result of seeing her again. "Every cloud."

"Cheers," she said, lifting her glass.

"To what," I asked, following suit.

"To your parents," she said. "May the Florida sunshine find them in good health and fine spirits."

"Thanks," I said, clinking my glass against hers. "I'll drink to that."

FIVE

- Laney -

He was even more handsome than I remembered.

Not that I tried to remember often.

If anything I did the opposite.

After all, I still believed breaking up with him was the biggest mistake of my life, which made it kind of weird to have small talk with him at my grandma's house over lemonade.

It was like no time had passed, and yet, at the same time, there was a tangible tension in the air between us.

I don't think the wall to wall crystals were making the whole thing any less surreal.

And there were so many questions I wanted to ask him, but the answers to those questions were none of my business any more. Or at least, the last time we'd spoken, I'd made it clear that he should go about his business without me.

I felt sick just thinking about it.

"What about you?" he asked.

"What about me?" I asked, wishing he would just talk, that he would just instinctively know all the questions I had and let me listen to his voice, a voice that at one time was the only thing I would've dropped anything to hear.

"Well I know you went to art school because your grandma told me."

I nodded. "I did, yeah. In Boston."

He raised his eyebrows. "And?"

"I loved it," I said. "It was the best thing I've ever done."

"And you're still there?"

"I've been in New York since I graduated," I said. "Because I like to make things extra hard for myself."

He smiled.

My heart didn't know if it should stop or skip a beat.

"What are you making lately?"

"Nothing," I said. "I'm cleaning up other people's art."

He tilted an ear towards me.

"Mostly the art that children make with the ingredients of their breakfast."

He nodded. "I see."

"It's only temporary, though."

"How long you been at it?" he asked.

"Almost two years."

He looked at me like he could see through all my bullshit. It was a familiar expression, one I hadn't seen in a long time but remembered well.

He used to make it a lot when we first met, when he'd sense that I was hiding things from him, which I was. But it wasn't personal. I was hiding things from everyone back then, myself included.

But he always got the truth out of me. Always. For better or for worse.

I don't know what it was about him that made me trust him with my most buried thoughts and hopes and secrets, but it was intoxicating to have someone in my life like that as a teenage girl.

Hell, it was probably intoxicating to have that at any stage in life, but I hadn't found it since.

In fact, I'd lied to Henry about everything. I don't know why. He probably could've handled the truth. I guess in the beginning it was just fun to be who I thought he wanted. He liked that version of myself and so did I.

But it wasn't authentic.

It was a show, a show I couldn't promise him I'd always have the energy to put on. And that was why I had to figure out how to break up with him when he'd literally never put a foot or a word wrong since I met him.

Though sometimes I wished he'd be a little bolder in the bedroom.

"So you aren't exactly using your degree?" Connor asked.

"What are you the degree police?"

"No. Sorry. I don't mean it like that," he said. "I just mean I'm surprised. You're such a fantastic artist."

I swallowed.

"I can remember walking along the beach in college and people would be doing the most amazing stuff in the street, and I'd always think 'I wonder what Laney's making right now.'"

"You thought about me? After you went away to school?"

He gave me a hard look. "I'm not even going to dignify that with a response."

"I think you just did," I said, trying to cut through the seriousness of his tone.

"You know damn well I thought about you."

I pursed my lips.

"You don't just think about someone every day for years- love someone every day for years- and then stop thinking about them overnight."

"I'm sorry, Con-"

"Save it," he said. "If you were sorry, you would've gotten in touch a long time ago."

A lump formed in my throat.

"But since you asked, cold turkey didn't work for me when things ended between us. And I couldn't exactly find a Laney patch to slap on my arm to help get you out of my system."

The gravity in his voice was uncomfortable. It made me wish all those screaming kids at the diner would run through the kitchen making airplane noises and spurting milk to break the tension.

He clenched his jaw. "You made promises you never intended to keep-"

"That's not true," I said, craning my neck forward.

"It is. But I'm over it."

I wasn't convinced, and I felt like a bad person for not being totally disheartened by that.

He drained the rest of his lemonade.

"Do you want some more?"

He raised a flat hand off the table. "No thanks."

"Is now a bad time to ask if you've met anyone special?"

He laughed. "I can see how you might think so, but you've asked now, haven't you?"

"Well?"

"I haven't done much dating since I left to be honest. It's hard to maintain a serious relationship when you're trying to become a vet in six years."

"How long is it supposed to take?" I asked.

"Eight."

"So why do it in six?"

He shrugged. "Stubbornness? I don't know. Patience isn't my favorite virtue."

I remembered the silly arguments we used to have over nothing. By the time the makeup sex was through, we couldn't even remember what we'd been fighting about.

"I did meet a lot of special animals, though."

I raised my eyebrows. "I bet."

"And I have a new puppy. Well, he's not technically a puppy any more. More like a difficult teenager."

"What kind of dog is he?"

"A golden retriever."

I smiled. "What's his name?"

"Sargent Pepper."

"Cute."

"He goes by Sarge, though," he said. "That is, if he's in the mood to take direction."

"I'd love to meet him."

"How long are you staying in town?" he asked.

"I'm not quite sure yet."

"Helly must be happy to have you."

"Yeah," I nodded. "She's the best."

"I lucked out with her as a neighbor anyway," he said. "She brought me a pie when I moved in, and she's brought over double chocolate brownies twice."

"Hence the tomatoes?"

"Hence me making sure I run regularly with my dog," he said. "What about you? Anyone special eagerly awaiting your return to New York?"

"Yeah. Sort of." Henry didn't even know I'd left yet.

Connor furrowed his brow.

"It's complicated."

I couldn't be sure, but I swore he glanced at my finger. It was the kind of thing I never would've noticed if I hadn't been so aware of that exact digit all morning.

"Well," he said, pushing his chair back. "I'll leave you to it."

I stood up, hating myself for selfishly wishing he wouldn't go. "Thanks for stopping by. I'll be sure to drop a hint that brownies would be very welcome payback for the tomatoes."

"Sarge and I are happy with pies, too," he said, heading for the door.

"Connor," I said when he pulled the door open.

He stopped and turned towards me.

"It was good to see you."

"You too," he said, stepping outside.

"And I'm sorry," I blurted.

"About what?"

"About before. About-"

45

"It's okay," he said. "Don't worry about it."

I felt hollow.

His mouth twitched. "All I ever wanted was for you to be happy."

But I wasn't. Couldn't he see that I wasn't? I hadn't been happy since-

"But if you insist on making it up to me-"

I craned my neck back, positive I'd suggested no such thing.

"Have dinner with me."

I tilted an ear towards him. "What?"

"Dinner," he said. "Have dinner with me."

"Can I think about it?"

"Come on, Laney. It's just dinner."

My lips fell apart.

"It's not like I proposed."

SIX

- Connor -

I tried to say it with good humor, but she flinched so hard I regretted it instantly.

And I was glad I hadn't verbalized the thought I had after the proposal comment, which was that I wouldn't make that mistake again.

It would only hurt her feelings.

Plus, it was a complete lie.

I didn't think proposing to her was a mistake at all.

I meant every word I said to her that day in the park, and I still meant it for months after she said no.

God those were the longest months of my life. Not only was she on the other side of the country, but she was gone from my life. Overnight.

I remember thinking it was some kind of cruel joke how jovial and sun kissed and smiley every surface of California seemed to be. Like the whole world was laughing at my broken heart.

It never even crossed my mind that she would say no.

But even now I was glad I asked. At least I didn't have any regrets about making sure she knew what she meant to me before I went, regrets I'd often wondered if she had.

Of course, I had to assume she didn't have any either. She never got in touch, never so much as poked me online. She didn't even have social media. Lord knows I checked.

I only wanted to know if she was okay.

Instead, it felt like she wanted me to know nothing, which is exactly what I knew. For years. Sure, my parents might've given me news if I'd asked. But after a while, it was just too sad to try and casually mention her.

I had too much pride to let others know how much she'd broken my heart.

But she knew.

She must've.

She had to have seen it in my face that day when I had a knee full of woodchips and the purest kind of hope in my eyes a man could have.

Until I asked her.

And not only did she say no, she said it was over.

It was a complete mindfuck.

After all, she was the girl who made me want things I thought other people were crazy for wanting. Like kids. And a mortgage. And staged Christmas cards. She was the one that made simple things amazing, the one who laughed hardest at my jokes, and the one I wanted to get old with.

I almost didn't accept my enrollment at UC Davis for her.

And she didn't even love me back. Not enough anyway. Not enough to justify how much those years meant to me.

She told me I was all she had more times than I could count.

But her actions forced me to wonder if it was just a line, if she'd just used me because she was the pretty new girl and knew that her beauty would be all consuming for a thirteen year old boy like me.

It didn't ruin me or anything.

My parents were living proof that true love existed.

If it weren't for them, though, my personal experience would be enough to give me doubts.

But seeing her again… It all came back.

All those nights she climbed the lattice work up to my bedroom window, all those nights we snuck out to go skinny dipping, all those classes we used to skip to have sex in my car.

She was my first everything. And at the time, my everything period.

But I was that for her, too.

I know I was. She told me so, and I could feel it in every bone in my body.

And I know love makes people stupid and crazy, but it felt good to be those things with her.

I would've bet anything then that we would've stayed that way forever.

But she had other plans, I guess. Plans I still didn't understand.

When she didn't say anything after I joked about the proposal, I told her she knew where to find me. Then I went next door and grabbed Sarge for a quick walk.

I couldn't bear the thought of sitting still in my house knowing she was just fifty yards away.

For years, I worked my ass off, knowing I'd come home eventually and hoping deep down she'd be back, too. But the reunion wasn't all laughs and hugs.

There were too many unanswered questions, too many unfelt feelings. Or felt in my case, but certainly not expressed.

And I'd let myself down for even letting her glimpse how much she'd hurt me. But she always had that effect on me.

She inspired me to want to become a man and yet, at the same time, her attention made me feel so safe I always ended up saying too much, feeling too much, and ultimately, wanting too much.

I had no business having nice thoughts about her, no business noticing how stunning she'd become, but it was like my mind and body weren't playing for the same side.

Logically, she was no good for me. She'd hurt me worse than I'd ever been hurt by anyone.

But I also knew she'd been hurt so much worse, and the fact that she ever even allowed herself to feel for me in high school was a miracle after what she'd been through.

So I couldn't hate her.

But I couldn't want her either.

And above all, I couldn't fall for her again when she'd so obviously moved on.

Besides, she wasn't entirely the person I remembered.

It was bizarre that she wasn't doing art any more. That fact alone made her sort of unrecognizable.

Still, I couldn't help but be curious about what went wrong. Why would someone with her gifts, her creativity, her eye for color and texture and light, settle for waitressing?

And the fact that she was still in New York?

Was Central Park really enough for her?

This was a girl whose favorite thing used to be walking barefoot through fields of wildflowers, laying in the tall grass, and talking about how wonderful it would be if we were wild lions stalking prey through the African plains.

Not that talking was the only thing we did in that grass.

But I couldn't quite put my finger on why she seemed slightly distant from herself.

The best way to describe it would be to say that she seemed a bit lost.

Right when I'd found her, ironically.

Worst of all, the stupid, stubborn, hopelessly sprung seventeen year old inside me spent the whole time I was with her jabbing me in the ribs so I would notice she wasn't wearing a ring.

And despite my best efforts to not give a shit, for some reason, it mattered.

SEVEN

- Laney -

What a mindfuck.

I decided then and there that I would never, ever get behind on my laundry again. A seemingly harmless quest for a clean pair of socks had chucked me into the weirdest morning of my life, and things were only getting weirder.

Again, I don't think all the crystals were helping.

After Connor left, I could barely make it back into the house before my legs collapsed, and I sat on the bench next to his tomatoes for who knows how long.

What were the chances of him being here? Today of all days?

And why did he have to look so good?

Why couldn't he have grown up to be a pimply hunchback whose teeth had gone to shit?

Why was his hair thicker than ever, his eyes an even darker blue? And was he taller? I mean, he was always tall, but I felt dwarfed by him in that worn grey sweatshirt.

For a few minutes, it was hard to understand what the hell I'd been thinking all those years ago. I remembered it like it was yesterday… the way he dropped to his knee in front of the swing I was swaying on, the hopeful sincerity in his eyes when he revealed the ring he'd pawned his golf clubs to buy.

Neither of us were ready for that kind of thing, but I know why he did it. He wanted me to know that just because he was going to pursue his dream in California didn't mean he didn't still want all those things we used to talk about.

And there was nothing he wouldn't have given me. He got me a duckling for my sixteenth birthday for crying out loud. Waddles. She used to follow me everywhere. She was as protective of me as a German Shepherd.

Until the day she flew away.

And I was no less interested in holding her back than I was in holding him, though pretending I wanted him to forget me was much harder to do.

But he was from a good family and had so much potential. Whereas I was a wannabe artist whose favorite mediums at the time were paper mâché and macaroni noodles.

And as much as he'd tried to put me back together, I was always going to have physical and emotional scars that would keep me from being the perfect girl he deserved.

I could tell by his face that he was shocked I'd said no.

When he finally stood up, there were woodchips hanging out of his knee.

That's when I realized I had no choice but to be even more firm. I knew he'd never believe me unless I was hurtful, nasty, and unapologetic.

So I was.

But seeing him again- even just remembering what it was like to be so physically near him- made me question everything I'd done.

Of course, it was too late.

And admitting to myself or anyone else that I wished I could go back and do things differently- like in the Choose Your Own Adventure Books I used to always make him read aloud to me- would make me look crazier than I already did in this house full of crystals and incense and tapestries that made me feel like I was backstage at Woodstock.

Ugh.

Besides, he wasn't the man I was supposed to be thinking about right now, the man whose feelings I was supposed to be considering.

But one thing- besides his ill-timed joke about how much easier it should be to accept a dinner invitation than a proposal – was niggling at me.

And that was the face he made when he realized I wasn't an artist any more.

The flash of sadness that swept across his eyes pissed me off. I mean, who the fuck was he to be disappointed in me?! If I didn't want to paint any more, why should he care?

Except maybe he knew what I often felt, which was that I kind of did want to paint… Every time I saw a chocolate chip pancake, every time I noticed a patch of graffiti, and every time I managed to hear a pigeon coo in downtown New York City.

Only I was sure I'd forgotten how.

Creativity for me was like a tap in the winter time. If you didn't turn it on regularly, it froze up.

And I hadn't turned the tap on since I left school and realized I had neither the personal funds nor the optimistic investors to justify my making art all day.

After all, I loved art, but I loved not starving to death even more.

I didn't even bring my paints when I moved into Henry's place. Looking at them drying in their bent tubes was doing nothing but making me sad.

But fuck Connor for noticing.

What I did or didn't do with my days wasn't his goddamn business, even if he was the first person who was ever genuinely interested in me and my wellbeing.

I was turning a tomato over in my hand- admiring how massive and smooth and shiny and red it was- when my phone started buzzing in my pocket. I pulled it out and swallowed.

"Hi," I said, with a tone of forced joviality that was neither comfortable nor appropriate.

"Hey- where are you?" Henry asked.

"I needed some fresh air," I said. "How was your day?"

"Fine. Landed a corporate gig that made me the hero of the office for a whole ten minutes."

"That's wonderful," I said. "Congratulations."

"I thought we might go out and celebrate. Maybe dinner at Cezanne's or something."

I never much cared for Cezanne. The artist, that is. The restaurant itself was fab, even though I hated the pretense of all that unnecessary cutlery. "Maybe we could raincheck that. I'm not really up for it tonight."

"We'll get whatever you want then. When will you be home?"

"I'm not coming home tonight, actually," I said. "I'm in Glastonbury."

"What?"

"I made the trip up this morning to visit my grandma."

"I'm sorry, babe. I must've forgotten you were planning to-"

"I wasn't. I just needed some fresh air."

"Is everything alright?" he asked. "You don't sound like yourself."

I took a deep breath and leaned back against the bench. "I'm fine. Just a bit tired."

"When are you coming back?" he asked.

"I don't know yet."

"What about work?"

"They were understanding," I lied.

"That's surprising."

"Mmm."

"Can you maybe narrow it down for me?" he asked. "So I know how many nights I'll be dining alone this week?"

I pinched the bridge of my nose and closed my eyes. "I can't yet."

"Do you want me to drive up there? You know I will if you want me-"

My eyes popped open. "No. Don't do that."

"Is your grandma okay?"

I nodded. "She's fine. Thanks for asking. I'll tell her you said hi."

"Sure you don't want me to come tell her myself?"

"I'm sure, honey. Don't be silly. You should get some sleep so you can be the office hero again tomorrow."

"I'll miss you tonight."

I leaned forward and stared at my toes. "Mmm."

"Love you."

I swallowed. "You too."

I hung up the phone and ran my fingers through my hair.

How was I going to explain to him that he wasn't the man for me? When he was such a good man? Such a kind man?

I should've just gotten it over with. Except we were too serious to break up over the phone. He deserved more than that. I loved him enough to at least give him that.

And tomorrow, God willing, the right words would come.

EIGHT

- Connor -

The summer moon lit up my childhood bedroom as I leaned in the doorway and looked around.

It was exactly as I'd left it all those years ago. What compelled my parents to leave it alone I'll never know, but I suppose the baseball inspired furniture- not to mention the wallpaper- made the space unsuitable for anything besides a boy's bedroom.

Plus, they didn't have the energy they used to.

Meanwhile, I didn't have the time. In the nine months since I'd moved in, I'd focused on updating the downstairs just enough to make it my own place without offending my parents on their next visit. But besides the master bedroom, which I'd completely refurbished, I'd changed very little.

I couldn't even remember the last time I'd come in my old room, much less let some air circulate, so I walked to the window and cracked it open.

The grassy smell of the summer air drifted in silently, breathing life back into the space.

Of course, I knew why I was in there.

It was because it reminded me of her.

And thinking about her was a distraction I wasn't trying nearly hard enough not to indulge in.

She used to climb up to my window on a strategically placed vine crawler.

Looking back, when I consider how many times my dad thought out loud about taking it down, I realize he must've known.

He probably left it there because he knew she'd find a way in whether he made it easy for her or not.

We weren't always up to no good though.

Sometimes she'd come over and simply ask me to read my Choose Your Own Adventure Books to her. She swore they were even more fun when I had to whisper.

And I adored how she'd never leave any stone unturned. She always wanted to know what all the adventures were, often making me go back two or three times to see how else the story could've turned out.

But our late night hangouts weren't always innocent either.

Despite the baseball wall paper and the little league trophies on the shelf, I became a man in this room- in more ways than one thanks to her.

Sometimes during an unbearably hot summer night, we'd sneak out and go down to the lake. I remember the first time we skinny dipped, how she pressed her cold nipples against my bare chest.

We were both still virgins then, but I didn't feel the same belligerent urgency to change that that my friends did. I wanted to lose my virginity, of course, but even then, I had this sense of calm- this certainty- that I had the rest of my life to sleep with her.

However, that's not to say it wasn't Earth shattering when it happened, though I realized pretty quickly that her Earth couldn't be shattered nearly as easily as mine.

But with a little practice, I got the hang of it.

I remember the first time she came for me. I remember how it felt to feel her charged body clench around me and melt. I'd never felt so alive, so sure in my purpose, so confident in my abilities as a man.

I admit I walked a little taller after that.

For four years, I embraced every single way she changed me.

And I watched her change, too. When she first moved to Glastonbury, she was effectively in pieces. Not that she was to blame.

In middle school and junior high, when my parents were supporting every goddamn sneeze I successfully caught with a tissue and writing embarrassing little notes for my lunch bag, she was going through hell.

It was bad enough early on for her, having a drunk for a mom who didn't even know who her real father was, much less where he might be found. But when her mom's boyfriend started getting out of line, she did everything she could to stay out of the way.

There wasn't an after school club she wouldn't feign interest in to keep from going home.

But soon the guilt of not trying to protect her mom ate away at her, and she started spending more time at the house. God knows she had the scars to prove it.

She was thirteen when she found out she had a grandmother living a few states away. She begged her mom to leave with her, begged her to acknowledge what a bad guy her boyfriend had become.

Instead of hearing her out, her mom called her names she could never bring herself to repeat.

She got on a bus the next day.

And I think that's why I was drawn to her. Because she gave off this energy that only people who are survivors give off.

It sounds crazy, but even though she'd seen more darkness than anyone I'd ever met in my thirteen years, she still managed to cast more light than I ever thought a person could.

And I basked in it every second I got, grateful for every corner of her soul she bared to me.

That was only one of the reasons I'd love her forever, though at the time I was falling, I didn't realize what a curse that love might become.

My phone buzzed in my pocket, and I reached for it without lifting my head off the ancient Yankees pillowcase.

"Evening friend."

"Billy Porter was a great call," Dave said. "The mayor loved the idea. Even the stupid sump pump bit."

I laughed and sat up. "Brilliant. I hope you took credit for it?"

"As if I'd give it to you."

"Good."

"I also inquired with the town council about the basketball court."

I raised my eyebrows. "Oh yeah?"

"They said there's a small pot of money that's supposed to go towards the renovations, but they don't have anyone to oversee the project."

"So it's been on hold."

"Yeah," he said. "For three years."

"Wow."

"So I put your name forward and said you were the guy to talk to."

I craned my neck forward. "Come again?"

"You can thank me later."

"Why would you do that?" I asked.

"Because you're the guy for the job."

I furrowed my brow. "How do you figure?"

"Because, stupid, that park is where Bark in the Park used to be held."

"I remember."

"So when we throw a grand re-opening of the park," he said. "We'll tell everyone to bring their pets."

"Pets don't play basketball."

"I'm aware of that," he said. "But I bet the grateful parents of basketball playing kids would be impressed to know that there's a new vet in town who loves kids as much as he loves animals."

"So, basically, you didn't want the job."

"I'd love to do it myself, but between the kids and the gangland warfare, I've got my hands full."

I sighed. "On a scale of one to ten, how much did you commit me to this?"

"You have a meeting with the mayor next week."

"Christ, Dave."

"Someday your children will thank me."

I wrapped my hand around my forehead. "I can't believe you did this."

"That's fine," he said. "Just make sure you believe it by nine o'clock Monday morning."

FLASHBACK
- Laney -

My first day of high school was the first day the contents of my lunch were ever a surprise.

I told my grandma that I could make my own lunch, that I'd been doing it since I was in second grade, but she insisted.

And there was a real note inside, written in her flowing cursive. It said she loved me and hoped I was having a nice first day of school.

It might've made me cry if I weren't so good at not showing weakness, sadness, and anything else bullies could smell that might make me a target.

I was used to getting picked on enough at home. I wasn't in the mood to deal with that shit at school.

But inside I was crying, crying and thinking about all those fake notes I'd written myself over the years so other kids might believe I had normal parents, too. Parents that didn't shout and break things and piss themselves.

I chose to sit alone that day.

Making friends wasn't a priority for me then. I suppose it never had been. Surviving was all that mattered. Surviving and making sure Grandma Helly and my teachers liked me so I'd never have to go home.

And I was ready to dine alone, too. I had a pretty book Helly gave me and, thanks to her note, I had a bookmark.

However, it was surprisingly hard to concentrate on the words with the hostile sounds of the unfamiliar cafeteria going on around me.

But I did my best, taking bites as I turned the pages.

And then everything changed.

Because the last thing I was ever expecting happened.

A handsome boy sat down across from me. "Hey," he said, popping his soda open.

I lifted my eyes from the page I'd been rereading for the sixth time.

He had sun kissed blond hair and blue eyes that were a much darker shade than mine. "Whatcha reading?"

"*I Capture the Castle.*"

"Never heard of it," he said. "Is it any good?"

"I don't know. I just started it."

"You don't recognize me, do you?"

I furrowed my brow and studied his face. "Should I?"

"I live next door."

"Oh."

"We're neighbors."

"Right." I prayed silently that he wouldn't ask me any of the questions I didn't want to answer, any of the questions that made me want to sit alone in the first place- like why I moved to Glastonbury and where I came from.

I didn't have answers to those questions that I liked, and the truth certainly wouldn't do. I could hardly tell this fresh faced, obviously loved kid that I was here because my mom's boyfriend broke a beer bottle over my arm when I got between them during a fight.

I couldn't say I arrived with a suitcase that had nothing in it but a box of perfectly sharpened colored pencils, three pairs of clean underwear, and a duckling stuffed animal I still slept with like a two year old.

He'd look at me like I was a two headed liar.

"What's your name?" he asked.

"Laney."

"I'm Connor."

"Nice to meet you."

"You want to walk home together after school?" he asked. "Since we're going the same way?"

"Sure."

"Cool," he said. "I'll meet you by the flagpole."

"Okay."

"You doing anything on Friday?" he asked.

I took a bite of my sandwich and covered my mouth with my hand. "Like what?"

"A few of us are gonna go down to the lake and have a bonfire."

I squinted at him. "Why are you telling me this?"

He swallowed the second to last bite of his sandwich. "I thought you might want to come. Since you're new and don't know anybody."

"Oh."

"Well?"

"Can I think about it?"

"Yeah, sure." He tossed the last bite of sandwich in his mouth.

There was something refreshingly unaggressive about him, something gentle, something that made me feel comfortable enough to lean forward so I could hear him better.

"Do you like lizards?" he asked.

"I don't know. Why?"

"Cause I have one," he said. "I could show it to you if you want."

"Okay."

"Who's your favorite superhero?"

I couldn't believe how nice it was to have someone ask me my opinion, especially about something so meaningless. "Batman, I guess."

"Batman?" He scrunched his face. "I guess you're not as smart as you look."

"Just because I have glasses doesn't mean I'm smart."

"I know," he said. "I like them, by the way."

I swallowed.

"But in case you're wondering, the correct answer is Spiderman."

"I didn't know there was a correct answer."

"You have much to learn," he said.

I laughed at his seriousness and the sound echoed through my body in a way I didn't recognize.

"Have you seen Spiderman 2?" he asked.

"I never saw the first one."

His eyebrows jumped up his face. "What?!"

I shrugged.

"Oh my god you have to see it. I have it. You can borrow it. Or we can watch it together. I never get sick of it."

"Okay," I said. "If you insist."

"I do insist," he said. "Urgently."

I laughed again and my heart lifted.

"Maybe we could watch it after school today," he said. "It's not like we'll have homework on day one."

"I'll have to ask my grandma."

"Helly?" he asked. "She's a huge Spiderman fan. She'll definitely be cool with it."

"She's a huge Spiderman fan?"

He nodded. "Maybe even bigger than me."

"If you say so."

The rest of lunch was full of surprises, all thanks to the handsome blond boy who talked to me like he'd known me for years.

Even when his friends called him over to their table, he waved them away with his hand and said we were in the middle of a serious discussion.

Which of course we weren't.

He was just telling me how lizards can regenerate their tails with an obscene enthusiasm I'd only felt once before when I got a free tiger spoon at the bottom of a bowl of Frosted Flakes.

But his passion was so awesome to witness I couldn't believe my luck.

We walked home together that day and watched Spiderman one and two.

And as I watched the scene with the upside down kiss, I felt a pinch in my guts and realized I wanted to be more than friends with the boy next door.

NINE
- Laney -

"Morning," I said, pushing the screen door open.

Helly was pottering around the garden with a basket full of weeds in one hand and a pruner in the other. "Morning," she said, bending over to yank something offensive out of the ground. "I thought you might want to sleep in."

"I tried," I said. "But my room is so sunny, and the birds are so loud. Lovely, but loud."

"As long as you're rested," she said.

I sat on the back stoop and set my tea down beside me. "I am."

"I've only got a few more fugitives to track down," she said, scanning the flowerbed at her feet. "Then I'm going to make you the delicious breakfast you refused yesterday."

"That sounds great."

"Oh- and I wanted to show you something," she said, chucking another weed in the flat basket.

"What is it?"

She set the basket down and wiped her hands on her thighs. "Come here."

I stood up and followed her over to the shed.

She pulled the metal latch to the left and swung the creaky red door open. "Ta da!"

"What's all this?" I asked, looking around. The first thing I noticed was my old easel at the back, which was covered by a familiar paint splattered sheet.

Next my eyes were drawn to several clear garbage bags lining the walls. The closest one was full of empty toilet paper rolls. Another was full of packing peanuts. Across the shed there were two more, one full of old newspapers and another with what appeared to be pieces of broken lawn ornaments.

Finally, I squinted at a bucket on the floor filled with broken shards of colored glass.

"It's stuff I've been saving for you," she said.

"For me?"

"Yeah," she said. "In case you get a hankering to make something crazy like you used to. I want you to know I'm prepared."

I furrowed my brow. "Are those broken lawn ornaments?"

"Are you opposed to working with new mediums?"

"Not opposed," I said, struggling to find the words. "I just haven't made anything out of junk since I was at school."

"It's only junk until you make something out of it," she said, stepping in the shed and spinning around as if she were in Aladdin's cave.

"It was very thoughtful of you to do this, Grandma."

She smiled. "Wasn't it, though? Remember when you made that life size chicken out of macaroni?"

"I do."

"And when you made that Rube Goldberg funnel that drained water into the cat's trough?"

I nodded. "That's another weekend I won't soon forget."

"I thought you might make a snowman with the packing peanuts," she said. "Wouldn't that be fun to have a snowman in the middle of summer?"

I pursed my lips. "I'm not sure the neighbors would love it if you put a trash statue in the yard."

"Who gives a scratch what they think? What matters is that you enjoy yourself."

She was so excited I wasn't sure how to let her down gently. How do you tell someone they've been wasting their time when they're inexplicably excited about the mundane trash they've been hoarding?

"I was thinking you could try making your own stained glass, too," she said, pointing at the bucket. "The stuff in the shops is so dated, and I'd love something for the back window in the sitting room."

I didn't know what to say.

"I don't expect you to get started on an empty stomach, of course," she said, stepping back onto the grass. "I just wanted to let you know this was all in here for you. And as always, I'm happy to get anything else you think you might need."

I glanced back at the easel once more. It looked smaller than I remembered and sadly neglected.

I stepped into the shed and lifted the felt parcel hanging off the top of it. Then I unrolled it and examined the brushes inside. I used to take such good care of them, and I'd be lying if I said they didn't call to me.

Because they did.

But at the same time, they didn't seem real. Or maybe I just wasn't ready to touch them for fear that I might lose myself under their spell like I used to so often. After all, there was a time when they made me feel like Harry Potter with his wand- unstoppable, optimistic, and full of untamable potential.

"It's nice that you kept all this stuff," I said.

"Of course," she said. "Your art used to bring me so much joy I can't even tell you."

"Me too."

"Your grandfather was an artist, you know?"

I nodded. "I remember you telling me."

"Right then. Let's get creative in the kitchen and gear up for the day ahead."

"Sounds good," I said, stepping back into the yard and closing the shed. It was such a confusing feeling to hear her belief in me.

Part of me wanted to forget about art- and for everyone else to forget what it once meant to me- and the other part wanted to dive back into the shed and not come out until I'd made a castle out of toilet paper rolls, painted it from top to bottom, and made stained glass windows for all the turrets.

I was following Helly in the house when I heard a car pull into the driveway.

"You expecting someone?" I asked, raising my eyebrows.

She shook her head and her voice dropped to a whisper. "No. Go see who it is, and if it's that lady from the church trying to raise funds so the priest can treat himself to new robes, tell her I've got whooping cough and that I'll call her when I'm no longer contagious."

"Seriously?"

"Seriously," she said. "And I'll go put the breakfast on."

"Okay," I said, heading around the corner.

"Laney," Henry said, closing his car door. He was standing in his suit, looking far too dressed up to be in such a pokey town.

"Henry. What are you doing here?" I asked, forcing a smile.

"I had to make sure you were alright."

I walked up to him and gave him a hug. "I'm fine."

"You sounded weird last night."

"I told you not to come."

"You also tell me not to make you two pieces of toast when I bring you breakfast in bed, but you never seem to mean it. So I don't know what to believe."

"But your work-"

"Can wait," he said. "For a few hours anyway."

I gave him another hug and held him tight. How was it that he always seemed to do the right thing?

Except when it came to picking me.

TEN

- Connor -

I was throwing a ball around the yard, trying to wear Sarge out so I could take him to work.

Not because I needed one more dog at the office, but because he ate half a slipper last night, and if his bowels went haywire later, I wanted to be there to lend a hand.

I'd just thrown the slobbery tennis ball for the hundredth time when I heard a man's voice next door, followed by Laney's.

Unfortunately, the tasteful bushes my parents and Helly had put between the properties forty years ago made it hard to see what was going on, and I couldn't hear well enough to make out the conversation.

But I had to know if he was Mr. Sort of.

When Sarge brought the ball back, he turned around before I threw it again, and when it didn't leave my hands, he turned around and looked at me like, "What are you stupid? I didn't bring you that so you could sit on it?"

I walked back towards the tall bushes and held the ball out. His mouth watered as he stared at it. "Now's your chance to get me back for the other day," I said. "So be a good wingman, and don't let me down."

He was nearly cross eyed from fixating on the ball.

I reached it over the chain link fence that went halfway up the bushes and let go.

He took off just how I wanted him to.

I followed him down the hedgerow and around the corner into Helly's driveway, feigning a slight jog despite the fact that I had no intention of hurrying once I arrived.

By the time I rounded the parked cars, Laney was already down on one knee, scratching him behind the ears and speaking to him at an elevated pitch.

The man in the suit stayed standing and was the first to see me coming.

"Sorry about that," I lied. "I'm trying to wear him out, but obviously it's my arm that's been the first to go."

Laney's eyes flashed up at me, and there was something unsettled in them. But when she looked back at Sarge, her expression changed again.

She stood up when he broke away and ran to me. "Morning."

"Morning." I looked back and forth between them. "Connor," I said, extending my hand to the suit.

"Henry," he said, shaking my hand.

The guy obviously had no idea who I was. "I live next door," I said, letting Sarge sniff him from the knees down while I sussed him out above the waist.

"Nice to meet you," Henry said, trying not to get slobbered on.

"Not a dog lover?" I asked.

"He's allergic," Laney said.

"So how do you know Laney?" I asked, allowing Sarge to keep doing his thing.

"I'm her boyfriend."

"Which one?" I asked.

The color drained from his face.

"That was a joke, man," I said, slapping him on the back a little too hard. "Lighten up."

"Aren't you late for work or something?" Laney asked me in a pointed tone.

"Not at all," I said. "But you're so thoughtful to ask."

She glared at me.

I tilted my head. "I think Henry might be, though. By the look of that suit."

Henry raised his eyebrows. "Is there something wrong with my suit?"

"No," I said. "Of course not. It's just a nicer suit than anyone my age would wear around here."

"Perhaps we're not the same age," he said, pointing out the obvious.

"Maybe that's all it is," I said. "How old are you?"

"Thirty six."

"That must be it then," I said. "What do you do, by the way? If you don't mind me asking."

"You must have somewhere to be," Laney said, her cheeks turning red.

"I'm an accountant," Henry said.

What the fuck was Laney doing with an accountant? She was raised by a crystal loving hippie for Christ's sake?!

"What about you?" Henry asked.

"I'm a vet," I said.

He raised his eyebrows. "A very friendly vet, I take it?"

I shrugged. "I try."

"Oh my," Helly said, coming around the corner. "I'm missing all the fun out here!"

"Grandma, this is Henry."

Helly gave Henry a big hug. "So nice to finally meet you. Don't you smell lovely?"

"And Connor was just leaving," Laney said, crossing her arms.

"Oh no," Helly said, turning to me. "Are you sure you can't stay? I've made far too much breakfast, and I used your lovely tomatoes in the omelets."

I smiled. "It's nice of you to offer, Helly."

"Too bad he can't accept the invitation," Laney said, her face twisted like a preteen who isn't getting her way.

"Laney's right," I said. "I really shouldn't stay, but I'd be a fool to say no. It's been far too long since I enjoyed one of your brunches."

Helly clapped her hands together. "Fantastic. Just give me a few minutes to set the table, and I'll call you guys in when I'm ready."

"Sounds good," I said, noticing Helly and I were the only ones that seemed pleased as she skipped away.

Henry angled his body towards Laney. "Any chance your folks are in town?"

"No," Laney said, avoiding my eyes. "They're traveling on business. As usual."

"Shame," Henry said. "I'm dying to meet them. Have you met them, Connor?"

I raised my eyebrows.

"A few times," Laney interrupted. "But he and my dad don't see eye to eye on politics so it always ends in an argument."

What the fuck was she talking about?!

"Isn't that right?" she asked, her eyes pleading with me.

"Yeah," I said. "Her dad's a real right wing nut job."

Laney hung her neck forward like I hadn't exactly aced the pop quiz.

"But her mom is definitely where she gets her good looks," I added. "I mean, talk about a milf-"

"That's enough, Connor," Laney said.

"I'm starting to think we'll just have to go visit them," Henry said. "If they're too busy to come to us."

"That's a great idea," I said. "They love visitors."

Henry let out the biggest sneeze I've ever heard. And right when I finally settled back into my startled skin, he did it two more times.

"Sorry, man," I said, taking a step backwards. "I'll get Sarge back inside and wash up for breakfast."

"Good idea," Laney said. "And if you can't come back, we'll understand."

"Oh I wouldn't miss it," I said.

Laney put a hand on Henry's square shoulder. "Why don't you go ask Helly for an antihistamine, and I'll be right behind you."

"Sure," he said, itching his eyes as he walked away.

I turned my back to them at the same time, but Laney poked me in the kidney as soon as I heard the front door close.

"What the hell, Connor?!"

I stopped in my tracks and faced her. "Excuse me?"

She put her hands on her hips and craned her neck forward. "Can you take a hint?"

"Can you tell me what the hell is going on here?"

"My boyfriend drove down to see me. That's what's going on here."

"So this isn't a joke?" I asked. "I was convinced I was dreaming this."

"It's not a dream. It's my life, asshole."

I fixed my eyes on her. "It's not your life, Laney. It's a charade." I threw the tennis ball into my own backyard so Sarge would stop breathing on my hand and watched him just long enough to make sure he got around the corner okay. "And Henry seems like an okay guy- not good enough for you, obviously- but you already know that-"

Her lips fell apart.

"But I bet he'd rather be in a relationship with someone who'd be real with him over whatever hilarious performance you're putting on-"

"It's not hilarious."

"No shit."

"Look," she said. "I don't expect you to understand but-"

"What could possibly justify the fact that he thinks you have parents somewhere that might want to meet him?"

She pressed her palm to her cheek.

"He probably thinks the scars on your arm are from Bark in the Park-"

Her whole body drooped.

"Oh my god. Tell me you didn't tell him you got bit by a dog."

"Please don't interfere."

"Hey, you're the one that started this joke," I said, raising my hands. "I just threw in a few punch lines on cue."

"It's not a joke," she said. "And I'm begging you to keep your mouth shut and not make this impossible for me."

"He has no fucking clue who I am, does he?"

She shook her head.

"What the fuck, Laney? Did what we had mean nothing to you?"

"Of course it did, but-"

"Breakfast is ready!" Helly called from the front porch.

"Please," she said. "I need to know you're not going to throw me under the bus."

I shook my head. "I'm not the guy that throws you under the bus, Laney. I'm the guy that lifts the bus off you after you jump in front of it. And frankly, I'm insulted by the fact that you haven't figured that out."

ELEVEN
- Laney -

The mischievous faced garden gnomes taunted me all the way back to the house, and by the time I sat down at the kitchen table, I wanted to die.

And strangle Connor, of course.

In just five minutes, he'd completely wiped away the guilt I felt over what I did to him and replaced it with frustrated rage.

I mean, it was cute when we hung out all the time when I was fourteen, but we were adults now, and I didn't appreciate him appearing out of nowhere when I was at my most desperate.

It was like he was some kind of predator that could smell my blood right before it got spilled.

And it was ridiculous for him to ask why Henry didn't know about him. As if the way to build solid relationships was to bring up the ex who popped my cherry, the ex who first made me feel like a woman, or the ex who made me believe I understood where Juliet was coming from when she stabbed herself with that happy dagger.

Ugh.

Not that I knew much about building solid relationships.

I'd only ever had one, really, and I blew it.

And apparently, it was still haunting me.

Meanwhile, my relationship with Henry was built on fabrications that resulted from my giving easy answers when I wasn't in the mood to be honest or open up. But my fibs were never supposed to hurt anyone. They were supposed to do the opposite.

Yet there I was on pins and needles wondering if Connor was going to use this opportunity as spiteful payback. After all, it would be so easy for him to break Henry's heart…

An hour before I intended to break it.

Fortunately, Henry seemed completely oblivious to the steam I could feel coming out of my ears, and Connor obviously thought he was at some kind of circus show because there's no omelet so tasty that it warrants a face as smug as the one he was making.

"So how did you two meet?" Connor asked, helping himself to a second serving of hash browns.

"I met her in the diner where she works," Henry answered between bites.

"How romantic," Connor said. "And who asked who out?"

"I asked her," Henry said. "I'm sorry, who are you again?"

"I live next door," he said. "Laney and I went to high school together."

"That's putting it a bit mildly," Helly said. "Don't you thi-"

"Does anyone want more tea?" I interrupted.

"No thanks," Connor said. "I'd rather save room for a few more hash browns. Helly, you've really outdone yourself."

"Yeah," Henry said. "I have to agree. These are way better than the ones at the diner, don't you think, babe?"

"Yeah," I said, pushing mine around the plate.

"So how long have you guys been together then?" Connor asked.

"You sure do ask a lot of questions for someone who almost didn't get invited to brunch," I said.

"Do you like the tomatoes, Henry?" Connor asked. "I grew them in my garden."

"Wow," Henry said. "I can barely grow my own toenails, much less something worth eating."

I forced a laugh that was so full of tension I was surprised no one offered me a laxative.

Then I started dominating the conversation with enough shit to clog every toilet in Glastonbury just to keep the two of them from speaking any more.

Finally, when everyone had cleaned their plates, Helly got up to do the dishes and Connor offered to help.

I thanked her again before excusing myself and Henry. Then I led him upstairs to my room and closed the door. I just couldn't take it anymore.

"Are you sure you're okay?" he asked, looking around my room and then back at me. "You're acting seriously weird."

"I'm not okay," I said. "I haven't been okay since you met me."

He laughed.

"I'm being serious."

He furrowed his brow. "What's going on," he asked, sitting on the edge of my paisley print bedspread.

"We need to talk."

"I kind of figured that out when you disappeared with a bunch of your stuff out of the blue yesterday."

"Right."

"Sit down," he said, patting the bed beside him. "And calm down."

I sat next to him and took a deep breath. He was so kind, so understanding. I never should've lied to him in the first place.

He probably would've loved me despite everything. But between my childhood and my being a waitress with no professional prospects, it seemed the least I could do was dip dye my past in some rose tinted paint.

I liked that he was so measured, so sturdy. I liked that he was older than me and thought my hysterics were cute, even though I didn't think they were cute.

I'd practically developed an ulcer the week I went to meet his parents at their house in the Hamptons. Sure, I'd proven that I could convincingly play the part of his girlfriend, but it would always be a part.

And if Harrison Ford could tire of playing Indiana Jones, how could I expect to be happy playing Henry Hart's other half forever?

"Talk to me," he said, lifting my chin.

I stared into his dark eyes.

"There's nothing you can't tell me."

I sighed. Apparently, there were loads of things I couldn't tell him, but none of them mattered now.

"Please, Laney. I have a lot of talents, but mind reading isn't one of them."

"I found the ring."

His eyes grew wide.

"In your sock drawer."

He swallowed.

"I can't marry you, Henry."

"I didn't ask."

"But you were going to," I said.

He nodded. "Someday. When I thought we were both ready."

"So why is there already an engagement ring in your sock drawer?"

"Besides the fact that I thought you wouldn't find it?"

I nodded.

"Because I saw it and thought it was perfect for you. And it was on sale."

I rolled my eyes. "You didn't have to add that last part."

"You didn't have to snoop in my sock drawer."

"I wasn't snooping," I said. "I didn't have any clean socks."

"Are you telling me the reason you freaked out and drove up here is because you found the ring?"

I shrugged. "I know it's ridiculous, but-"

"Ridiculous isn't the word I would've used."

I raised my eyebrows.

"Worrying," he said. "That's the word that came to my mind."

"I know."

He brought his hands together and looked down at his lap.

"It's not that I don't love you."

"You just don't love me enough."

"No."

He looked at me. "And you don't think you ever will?"

"I'm sorry."

He nodded and stared at the purple shag carpet in the middle of the floor.

"Isn't it better that I told you sooner rather than later?"

He cocked his head. "It would be better if you loved me back."

"I do love you."

He fixed his eyes on me. "Just not the way I love you."

I pursed my lips.

"I can't believe this is happening."

I desperately wanted to open a window, but it didn't seem like the moment to leave his side.

"Why would you move in if you didn't want a future with me?" he asked.

"I thought I did."

He narrowed his eyes. "Until you found the ring?"

I nodded.

"Was it the princess cut? Would you prefer a marquise-?"

"It's not the ring, Henry. And it's not you. It's me. Really."

It's always me.

TWELVE

- Connor -

I couldn't believe she did her fake laugh for that guy. I'd totally forgotten she did that, and now it was haunting me.

And I know I didn't imagine it. It happened too many times. So what the fuck was she doing with him?

Sure, he seemed alright, but she was a free spirit, and he was obviously a stick in the mud compared to her.

Maybe she'd changed. Maybe she wasn't the Laney I used to love. Maybe I'd dodged a bullet.

And yet, despite the weirdness of her behavior since she arrived, deep down I was still convinced I knew her better than anyone.

"Same again," Timo asked?

"Sure," I said, checking my watch.

"Dave meeting you?" he asked, filling a fresh glass.

"He's supposed to be." I drained the last of my beer and slid it to his side of the bar.

"Must be on Dave time."

I nodded. "As usual."

Timo set a pint of Daisy Cutter on my cheap coaster and went to attend to some local fireman across the room who were downing pitchers faster than they were breaking darts.

I looked at the door and then back at my drink. It wasn't just the fake laugh that was bothering me. It was the fact that Henry was obviously into her, and she'd clearly been lying to him as she saw fit.

The whole display made me feel kind of sick. Not because his well-being was any of my concern- the guy looked reasonably capable of looking after himself- but because I couldn't say for certain that I hadn't been just as much of a schmuck.

For all I knew, I was that guy.

After all, there was no question I was blinded by love back then, but what if everyone around me could tell she didn't care about me as much as I cared about her. Was that even possible?

I clenched my jaw.

If it had all been a show, she'd duped the shit out of my parents, too. And my friends. Right? It wasn't just me. It couldn't have been. The love I felt for her was still the most real thing I'd ever felt.

And if it wasn't real, didn't that make me some kind of crazy person?

"Sorry I'm late," Dave said, sliding onto the barstool next to me.

"It's fine," I said. "But you've got some catching up to do."

"What'll it be, Dave?" Timo called from the far end of the bar.

"Whatever Connor's drinking and some chili cheese fries."

Timo nodded and went to the small window that opened into the kitchen.

"Chili cheese fries?" I asked.

He nodded. "It's meatloaf night."

I furrowed my brow. "So you're deliberately spoiling your dinner?"

"It's not real meatloaf," he said. "Amber's gotten all into this turkey tasting soya bullshit."

"I don't know what that means."

"It means you could dribble her meatloaf like a basketball."

"Do the kids like it?" I asked.

"Only cause they don't know any better," he said. "And because they'll eat anything that tastes like ketchup."

I swallowed a sip of my beer. "Does she always make healthy stuff?"

"She didn't used to," he said. "She used to delight the whole family with chicken nuggets and fish sticks and all the other things that taste like happy childhoods."

"So what changed?"

"I don't know. Some queen bitch told her about the healing properties of quinoa and kale and now everything has gone to shit- literally."

"Have you told her how you feel?" I asked.

He looked at me like I had six heads. "Do I strike you as the kind of guy that sits his wife down to discuss his feelings about kale?"

"There's a right answer to this question, isn't there?"

He nodded as Timo brought his beer and got stuck straight into it. "God that's good."

I smiled.

"Heard you had breakfast at Helly's?"

I tilted an ear towards him. "How do you know that?"

"Saw her at the post office," he said. "For a second I thought she was trying to sell me your tomatoes."

"They are good ones."

"She told me Laney's in town."

I nodded.

He raised his eyebrows.

"What?"

"How is she?"

I shrugged. "She seems out of sorts. Not that I would know what her normal sorts are these days."

"Uh-huh."

"And she's stunning as ever, unfortunately."

He shook his head. "That's what I was afraid of."

"Why?"

"You should stay away from her, man."

I cocked my head. "Excuse me?"

"Don't you remember how she put you through the ringer?"

My grip tightened around the cool base of my glass. "We were kids then."

"Not if I was old enough to make kids then."

"It's not like I can't be around her. It's not like I'm still in love with her."

He fixed his eyes on me.

I craned my neck back. "What?"

"You're playing with fire, Connor."

"I'm not playing with anything."

He sighed. "Well, she is."

"Sorry?"

"She's playing with your emotions," he said. "I don't even have to see you together to know that."

"She's doing no such thing."

"She kept you from thinking straight for four years. Don't you think that's enough time to waste on her?"

"None of those years were wasted, Dave."

He scoffed. "Whatever. She can't be trusted."

"I'm not trusting her with anything."

"Good," he said. "Because I hate to be harsh, but she's not like us. I gave her the benefit of the doubt back then, but what she did to you showed her true colors."

"I don't think it did."

"What the fuck? Can you even hear yourself? Of course it did."

I shook my head. "I don't think that was her."

"Which part wasn't her? The part where she broke your heart or the part where she made it clear for months afterwards that she wasn't sorry about it?"

I swallowed.

"That's what I thought." He lifted his glass. "She's not the girl for you, man."

"Then who is?"

"I don't know... Tiffany Ascot? Emily Wilson? One of the Detgens?"

I rolled my eyes.

"What?"

"None of them do anything for me."

He craned his neck forward. "None of the Detgens do anything for you? What are you on animal drugs?"

I laughed. "Yes. Didn't you know? That's why I really became a vet. So I could pop worming tablets and give myself flea treatments."

"Don't be a smartass," he said. "I'm only trying to help."

"I don't need help."

"Maybe not, but you do need to keep moving forward and not look back, especially in the direction of Helly's house when Laney's there."

"I think she's in trouble."

"She's always in trouble! That's how she gets you. Can't you see that? She's a user."

"Don't talk about her like that," I said, taking a swig of beer.

He rolled his eyes. "Oh please. She's not your girlfriend any more. It's not your job to defend her honor."

"I never thought it was my job. I thought it was a fucking privilege."

He groaned.

"I was thinking of bringing her to the barbeque if she's still in town."

He squinted at me. "Why would you do that to yourself?"

I shrugged. "She might like to see some old friends. I bet Amber would like to see her."

"She didn't just turn her back on you, Connor. She turned her back on everybody."

"No she didn't. She just went off to college like the rest of us."

Dave flinched.

"Some of us," I corrected. "But I'm not going to bring her around if you're going to be an unwelcoming jerk."

"I'm not going to be a dick to her. You know I'd be her best friend on Earth if you asked me to be, but I'm also not going to lie to your face and tell you I think letting her back into your life is a good move."

"Good thing I don't need your permission."

Dave shrugged. "Just tread carefully, man. Fool me once as they say."

I couldn't argue with that. It was true I'd been a fool for her.

But as much as she hurt me, I couldn't forget the good times.

And I didn't want to.

Besides, it's not like I was going to fall for her all over again.

The Boy Next Door

THIRTEEN
- Laney -

I loved that little twin bed.

It was like a coffin in the best sense, just big enough for me and my racing thoughts.

Suddenly, I sat up and reached for my phone.

The busy clatter of the noisy diner answered the phone even before Edy did.

"Edy, it's Laney."

"Hi."

"Can I talk to Warren?"

"Ummm."

I waited while she looked around.

"Yeah, hold on a second."

I ran my fingers through my hair.

"Make it quick, Laney," he said when he got on the phone.

"I quit," I said. "That quick enough for you?"

"You can't be serious-"

I hung up to show him that I was, and I felt equally hysterical and elated as soon as I'd done it.

Then I decided I would allow myself to feel good about no more dirty plates and rude customers and being sniffed by strange dogs because of the bacon smell in my clothes and pores.

And under no circumstance would I fret about having no income and no job and no clear direction.

Not yet.

Not for at least two whole minutes.

"Come in," I said when I heard Helly's soft knock on the door.

"I brought scones," she said, pushing the door open with her hip. "And homemade jam."

"Amazing," I said, scooting to the edge of the bed.

"Remember how I used to bring you fresh scones when you'd sulk in your room as a teenager?" she asked, laying the tray on my child sized desk.

"I do."

"And how you used to tell me everything?" she asked, handing me a plate of jam filled scones.

I laughed. "That's not quite how I remember it, but I suppose I might've told you a few things."

Her kind eyes smiled. "Are you ready to talk about this morning?"

"I need to ask you something first."

She pulled the simple wooden desk chair out and sat down. "Go on."

"Can I stay here for a while?"

She raised her eyebrows.

"I hate to ask a favor of you when you've already done so much for me, but-"

"Don't be silly," she said. "Of course you can stay."

I felt my chest loosen. "Thanks, Grandma."

"You're welcome. You remember the house rules?"

"No cats inside and no crystals out?"

She nodded. "And no blowing dandelions in the yard."

"Right."

"Even if they are your favorite."

I smiled.

"You can blow them in Connor's yard, though," she said. "Something tells me he wouldn't mind."

"Connor's a pest," I said. "And you shouldn't have invited him to breakfast."

She tilted her head. "Really? I think it's that other young man I shouldn't have invited."

"Henry?" I asked, breaking off a piece of warm scone.

"Yeah," she said. "He's the one that ran over the mailbox on his way out."

My eyes grew wide as I chewed. "What?"

"You want to tell me what would make such a put together guy back over my mailbox?"

"I broke up with him."

She nodded. "That explains why he told me 'thanks for breakfast and goodbye forever' right before it happened."

"I'm so sorry."

"Don't be. It's just a mailbox," she said. "Plus, the postman got a great laugh over how I tried to prop it back up. He came to the door and asked if he could meet the hobbits who were living here."

I covered one eye with my hand.

"Then he helped me put it in one of my old milk cans so it would be high enough for him to reach it from his truck next time," she said. "And I think it's actually an improvement."

"I'm so glad something good could come out of me breaking up with my boyfriend."

She dropped her chin but kept her eyes on me. "I think it was a good thing anyway, dear."

"You didn't like him?" I asked, taking another bite and relishing the way the fresh raspberry spread burst against my tongue.

"No. He was alright. I just didn't like you with him."

"What?"

"I hardly recognized you with the amount of lies coming out of your mouth."

My shoulders sagged.

"Not to mention the fact that I've obviously gotten zero credit for raising you."

"You know I'm not proud of my past."

"That's no excuse to lie to someone like that," she said. "That poor man thinks he broke up with Laney Price this morning when all he did was break up with some character you were playing."

"It was a mistake, okay? He's just from such a normal family-"

"There's no such thing," she said. "And I still love you to bits, but you let yourself down."

"I know, but it was never my intention to hurt him. I just liked pretending to be the kind of woman who was good enough for a man like him."

She raised a flat palm between us. "That's absurd, Laney. Who you are is good enough for anyone."

I swallowed.

"Besides," she said. "Honesty is everything in a relationship."

"I know. You've been saying that for as long as I've known you."

"And three hundred years before that, if you can believe it."

I smiled.

"Do you know what happens when you let lies poison your relationships?"

"Tell me."

"Well," she said, pouring two cups of tea. "You know what happens to a glass of milk after you dunk an Oreo in it?"

"Of course."

"You know how every time you dunk another Oreo in, the milk becomes darker and darker?"

I nodded. "I do."

"That's what lies do to a relationship. They muddy it until it's unrecognizable."

I pursed my lips.

"And there's no going back," she said, handing me a cup of tea on a saucer. "You can't get the lies out once they're in."

"So I've learned."

"How are those scones?" she asked.

"Good enough to spoil my dinner."

"I was hoping," she said. "I'm not in the mood to mess up the kitchen again today. I thought we'd have scones for dinner and popsicles for dessert."

"I'm cool with that."

"I thought you might be," she said. "Now get stuck into that other one while I tell you a story."

"I was going to let you eat that one."

She shook her head. "I already had too many, and at this age, the skin on my neck doesn't bounce back the way it used to so I'm cut off."

I laughed.

"If you catch me reaching for any later, just start mooing at me, and I'll take the hint."

"I'm not going to do that."

She cocked her head. "I would do it for you."

"Fine," I said, reaching for the second scone. "Tell your story."

"Your grandfather wasn't my first."

I raised my eyebrows.

"There was a guy before him. He was in the navy."

"You were a sucker for a man in uniform, huh?"

"Who isn't?" she said. "I'm only human."

"Go on."

"I was crazy about this guy, Laney. I dreamt of having little boys who could grow thick mustaches just like he had."

"So what happened?" I asked.

"I realized he wasn't good for me long term... though he was very good short term, if you know what I mean."

"So what was the problem?"

"I thought I wanted someone I could be anyone with," she said. "And he made me feel like that. Like I could be anyone I wanted."

123

"Uh-huh."

"But what I thought I wanted wasn't what I needed."

I covered my full mouth. "What did you need?"

"Someone I could be myself with."

I swallowed my bite of scone.

"You see, life is short if you're living it right," she said. "But if you spend your days pretending to be someone you're not, it can feel very long."

I took a sip of tea.

"And you can take it from me because I've tried it both ways."

I wrapped my palms around the steaming cup. "Why are you telling me this?"

"To make sure you get it right this time around… And because it crossed my mind, and I'm at that age where I have to say stuff when I think it or my thoughts disappear with the fairies."

"Right."

"Speaking of which, will you do me a favor?"

"Of course."

"Will you remind me I need to update my will this week?" she asked.

"You're changing your will?"

She nodded. "Just one teeny detail."

I raised my eyebrows. "What's that?"

"When I'm buried, I want your grandfather's urn between my legs instead of up by head."

I furrowed my brow. "Why?"

"Because it's been too damn long since he was there."

FOURTEEN
- Connor -

I let Sarge lick my plate and then stuck it in the dishwasher.

He made puppy eyes at me in a bid for of another lick, but his expression lifted again when he heard the doorbell ring.

He ran for the front door, his paws sliding against the floor as he rounded the corner while his tail wagged so hard I thought he might take off.

"Let's hope it's not an intruder," I said, following after him. "Or you're out of a job, buddy."

It looked like Laney's outline in the blurred glass, but I was worried my mind might be playing tricks on melike when you think you see a quarter on the ground but it's just a spot of gum.

But it was her.

"Laney."

"Hi." She was holding a plate of scones covered with light pink Saran wrap.

Sarge wiggled out past my legs and planted his paws on her thigh.

"Would you like to buy a scone?" she asked, reaching a hand down and scratching one of Sarge's golden ears so good he pressed his face against her leg.

I smiled. "Depends on how much they are."

"One hundred dollars for the plate," she said. "Or you can have an apology, and I'll throw them in for free."

"In that case," I said, stepping backwards and opening the door wider. "Allow me to make some room for the apology."

She stepped in the house and looked around. "Wow."

Sarge kept sniffing the air as if scone crumbs might fall like snowflakes any minute.

I closed the door, letting my eyes fall from her narrow shoulders down to the cropped jeans that hugged her ass in a way I wished I hadn't noticed.

"I'm ready," I said when she turned around.

She pushed some stray blonde wisps out of her face. "I want to apologize for the way I treated you this morning."

"Great. Can I have the scones now?"

"I'm being serious."

"So am I," I said, noticing the simple earrings she was wearing. I always liked that part of her just below her earlobe. The first time I tickled that spot with my stubble was the first time I felt my stubble was good for anything. "Besides, it's not me you owe an apology," I said, taking the plate from her and walking into the kitchen.

She followed behind me in her bare feet, losing my dog's attention once I had the scones. "Yes it is. I was rude. And you didn't do anything wrong."

I shook my head and pulled a scone out from under the thinly stretched Saran wrap. "No it's not. It's Henry, the poor guy. I've felt bad for him all day."

She folded her arms.

I could tell she was trying to focus on the conversation despite wanting to look around and see all the updates I'd made to the place. It was modern and bright and my mom's collection of painted plates had been replaced by a forty inch TV.

"I already apologized to him," she said, standing behind a barstool without sitting down. "Not that it's any of your business."

I pulled out a small plate and opened the fridge.

"Helly said you should have them with the raspberry jam she gave you, and I can second that since we had scones for dinner."

I found the jam in my fridge and turned around. "You know he's all wrong for you, right?"

Her mouth twitched.

"And that's not coming from some relic of teenage jealousy," I said. "It's the truth."

Her face started to turn red.

"Your whole relationship is a joke," I said, slicing the scone. "You even did your fake laugh at him."

"I did not."

"You did," I said, spreading some butter on the bottom half. "At least three times."

She furrowed her brow. "You were counting? What the hell is your problem?"

"How much time you got?" I said, glancing up at her. "All I know is one of my problems isn't that I'm in a relationship with someone who thinks I'm someone I'm not."

"Fuck you."

I dropped some jam in the scone and spread it around.

"Who the fuck do you think you are?" she asked. "I haven't seen you in years-"

"Whose fault is that?"

"And you think you can tell me how to run my life?!"

"No offense," I said, closing the scone. "But it doesn't seem like you're doing a very good job." When I looked up, her eyes were glassy and her bottom lip was shaking. "Jesus, Laney, I didn't mean-"

"Yes you did," she said, dragging a finger under her eye.

"I'm sorry," I walked around the butcher block to where she was standing. "I shouldn't have said that. I had no right-"

"No," she said, her eyes full of pain. "You didn't."

I put a hand on her shoulder.

"But you're not wrong," she said.

"No, I am. I shouldn't have-"

"I've made a mess of things," she said.

"What mess?" I pulled out a barstool and gave her a nudge.

She sat on it and put her elbows on the counter, still keeping the tears from spilling from her eyes.

"What's going on?"

"It's over," she said.

"What is?" I pulled out the barstool beside her.

"Me and Henry."

It took everything I had not to smile, and I felt like a piece of shit for not being able to be more genuinely sympathetic.

"And my job."

I raised my eyebrows. "Your job?"

"I quit."

"It was just a job," I said.

She looked at me for the first time like maybe I did understand, like maybe I was on her side. "You're right. It was just a job. That must be why I don't feel worse about it."

"You couldn't stay there forever."

She leaned back. "It was killing me."

"And I'm sorry about Henry."

She shook her head. "No you're not."

I pursed my lips.

"It's okay," she said, catching my eye. "I know you didn't like him."

"I didn't like him for you," I said.

"I did." She shrugged. "I liked him a lot. And I liked myself with him."

She might as well have wiggled a blunt knife into my gut.

"Or the version of myself I was with him, anyway."

"Exactly what version of yourself was that?" I asked.

"The small part of me that's ready and willing to be an adult."

I laughed. "Being an adult is overrated."

She leaned her head back and blinked to absorb her tears. "Overrated but mandatory."

"You can still keep that side of you if you liked it," I said. "It's not like he took it when he left."

"I don't know if I want to," she said. "I don't know what the hell I want."

"That's okay, you know."

"No it's not."

"Everyone's faking it, Laney. No one has everything figured out."

"Some people do."

"I wish that were true," I said, reaching across the counter to slide my plate over. "Then the rest of us would have something to aspire to."

"I guess I just wish I could rewind a few steps. Like in a Choose Your Own Adventure Book."

"So do that."

"I can't," she said. "It's too many pages back where I took a wrong turn."

"When would you want to go back to?"

She rolled her eyes up to the ceiling. "How about that day we stole the Disaronno from your parent's liquor cabinet?"

I scrunched my face. "Can't we go back to a day when we got our hands on something that was actually drinkable?"

She laughed.

"That was the first time my dad didn't punish me for stealing booze. He said we did him a favor."

"Really?"

I nodded.

"Fine," she said. "What day would you pick?"

FIFTEEN
- Laney -

I watched him chew as he mulled it over.

"Well?"

He swallowed. "There are so many good days to choose from."

"I didn't come over here to ask easy questions."

"And here I thought you just came bearing innocent scones, no tricky questions attached."

"Tough," I said. "What'll it be?"

He squinted, his deep blue eyes inhaling my attention. "Maybe the day I gave you Waddles?"

I smiled. "Why that day?"

"I think that was one of the funniest days of my life. Watching you try to imprint on that duckling was beyond hilarious. You turned into a total schoolmarm."

My mouth fell open.

"I laughed so hard my eyes watered, and I could feel the stitch I got in my side for two days afterwards."

"I loved that duck."

He smiled, little creases springing around his eyes. "She loved you, too."

"That was the best present ever."

"Who knew the present of complete adoration could come so cheap?"

"And complete protection," I said. "Remember when she charged after Dede Vedder's German Shepherd when it snatched my ice cream sandwich?"

"You did drop it two feet away from him."

I craned my neck forward. "I was going to pick it up."

"Yeah, well, the five second rule is no good with a German Shepherd around."

"Well, I haven't made that ice cream dropping mistake since," I said, raising a finger. "Just in case you think I'm not capable of learning from my mistakes."

"I don't think that."

"Good."

"Sometimes I just think it takes a whole helluva lot longer than it should," he said. "But you were in the slow math class so-"

"And honors everything else, jackass."

He rolled his eyes. "I remember."

"And if math grades were based on how pretty your work was when you had to show it, I would've been head of the class."

"So true," he said. "I still have no idea why rainbow colored bubble letters don't make up for incorrect algebra."

I punched him in the arm, and a lump formed in my throat when I realized how solid it was. It was nothing like punching his eighteen year old arm, anyway, and I felt my whole body go up in goosebumps at how foreign he suddenly seemed. "I'll have you know I've never needed any of that stuff."

"And I've never needed French."

I raised my eyebrows. "Not even to talk to French Poodles?"

He laughed.

The low sound vibrated in my bones.

"I wish I could talk to my patients," he said. "That would make my job a thousand times easier."

"Helly told me you're pretty good at it anyway."

"Helly's biased."

"Sure, but sometimes she's right," I said. "She told me you invented a revolutionary wine stopper."

He groaned. "It's not a wine stopper. It's an artificial foot to help three legged animals walk again."

I tilted my head. "I thought animals were fine on three legs?"

"They are. But depending on when and how they come to have three legs, sometimes it's less traumatic for them to get a replacement."

"That makes sense."

"I'm still waiting on the patent to come through, though. Could be a game changer."

"Especially if that game is animal double dutch."

"Good one," he said.

"So you like it as much as you always thought you would?"

"I do. But I've always known what I wanted," he said, looking away from me.

I swallowed. "This place looks great, by the way. It's totally transformed."

"Only this space is," he said, gesturing between the open kitchen and the attached living room. "And the master bedroom."

"Oh."

"I'll get to the other rooms eventually," he said. "But this area needed the biggest makeover."

"I see you've decided to do away with your mom's plate collection?"

He popped his last bite of scone in his mouth.

I raised my eyebrows. "I take it they weren't bachelor pad enough for you?"

He swallowed. "No. And you didn't even see how weird the collection got the last few years."

"Really?"

He nodded. "Let's put it this way, I don't know if she was more into Princess Diana or Muhammad Ali."

"Are they worth anything?"

"Unless they start literally floating like butterflies and stinging like bees on their own, I'd be surprised if they're worth the money she paid for them."

"So you didn't sell them to help pay for that ridiculous TV?" I asked.

"It's not ridiculous," he said. "If I put some visually decadent movie on there, you'd think it was the best thing you'd ever seen."

"Perhaps."

He stood up and set his plate on the floor so Sarge could lick a few crumbs and blobs of jam. Then he carried his plate to the dishwasher. "So are you going to stay in Glastonbury for a while then?"

"Looks like it," I said. "Until I figure out what to do next?"

"And what are your options?"

"Anything and nothing."

He raised his eyebrows. "So you're free for dinner?"

I felt my stomach somersault in a way that felt good and wrong at the same time.

"Or did you have your heart set on having scones with your grandma every night?"

"I suppose it would be adult of me to try and make time for some other food groups."

He lifted his large hands. "I can't comment one way or the other. I'm not the authority on appropriate adult behavior."

"Really? Cause it seems like you've got your shit together."

He craned his neck back. "Why? Because I have a roof over my head?"

"And a good job."

One corner of his mouth curled up. "Now that you mention it, I suppose I am a pretty good catch."

A sickening wave of regret crashed in my stomach.

He set his hands on the opposite side of the counter. "Did you want something to drink?" he asked. "I should've asked before-"

"No, I'm okay. Thanks, though."

"Don't be shy," he said. "I've got just about everything."

"A good catch would," I said.

He cocked his head. "Are you making fun of me?"

"Not at all. Just trying to figure out why someone like you doesn't have a barefoot, pregnant wife creeping around."

"Maybe I do," he said.

"Well, she's very quiet."

"That's what I like best about her," he said. "Even the kids are silent."

"Sounds like a dream come true."

His face twitched like he didn't agree.

143

"Seriously, though, why are you still single?"

"Why are you?" he asked.

"Because I'm a complete head case."

"No you're not."

"Have you just not met the right girl?" I asked.

"That's definitely not it."

"So what do you suppose the reason is?" I asked. "You must have some idea. You've always been pretty self-aware."

He folded his arms.

"Well?"

He fixed his eyes on me. "Let's discuss it over dinner."

"Why do you want to have dinner so bad?"

"Because," he said. "I think you owe me that much."

SIXTEEN
- Connor -

I let Sarge outside for a few minutes and hid all the shoes in the house. Then I got dressed, keeping it casual but taking into consideration the kind of stuff Laney used to like.

For example, I knew she didn't care for black shoes and that she thought I looked great in blue. Or at least she once did, though the fact that I remembered which shade was as disturbing as it was surprising.

After all, why wouldn't something else have moved into my headspace where all those little details about her once lived... like which Spice Girl she liked best, the fact that she liked grapes but not grape flavored things, and the fact that she could never remember Schubert's name but would be struck still by his music every time, as if she could hear it on a frequency other's couldn't, as if it were written for her in a past life.

I didn't want to remember that stuff.

And still, I pulled on a white and blue collared shirt because my hand wouldn't let me pick the red one.

It was so stupid.

Even taking her out to dinner was stupid. And I knew it. Just like Dave said.

Running into her again was like finding a genie's lamp that once delighted you before it got you into loads of trouble. And yet, who wouldn't rub a genie's lamp again? Just to see what was in store. Just because life was more interesting with surprises.

At least I hadn't lost the run of myself and made ridiculous reservations at some fancy restaurant. That would be presumptuous. And awkward. And not just because we'd never been to a fancy restaurant in our lives.

I'd dreamed of taking her somewhere she could get a decent steak or a desert so chocolatey that her eyes would roll back in her head and she would moan like she did when my hands were on her.

But it never happened.

Partly because she thought silverware was a poor substitute for fingers, and partly because- by the time I had enough money saved to take her somewhere nice- I already knew I wanted to buy her a ring.

But despite the casual dining habits we had, I was proud of the reputation I'd earned of being her favorite gift giver.

Waddles was probably my best, but I used to get her loads of art supplies and fancy wigs, too. She used to love fancy wigs. She'd wear them to parties in high school and pretend she was different characters all the time.

As amusing as I thought it was, sometimes I'd suggest she let people get to know her instead of acting so crazy. But she said the wigs helped her be herself, not the other way around. Other times, she'd whisper in my ear that she didn't want to share her real self with anyone but me.

It was intoxicating.

So I kept spending my pocket money on wigs because I didn't give a shit what anyone thought as long as she was happy.

When I'd freshened my breath to the point that it smelled like I'd swallowed a forest full of pine trees, I called Sarge back in and left the house.

She opened the door in a wig.

I smiled. "I like you as a brunette."

"This is the one I wore on Halloween, remember? The year I begged you be John Smith."

"Because you didn't recognize the brilliance of my Spiderman costume."

"No. Only the tightness."

I raised my eyebrows. "I thought you liked it."

"I did," she said. "Until we had to leave the party because of it."

"Can't say I remember you complaining at the time."

She blushed, dropped her head, and pulled off the wig.

That's when I noticed she was wearing a little blue wrap dress that made her eyes pop.

"I still have them all," she said, throwing the wig on the bench inside the door and pulling it closed behind her. "Guess how many?"

"Eight."

"Fourteen!" she said, her eyes wide.

"Are they getting much wear these days?" I asked, stepping off the stoop.

She shook her head. "That's the first one I've put on in years."

"Still a thrill?"

She shrugged. "Sort of. But I'd rather be myself tonight."

I glanced down to make sure she was wearing comfortable shoes. Not that I needed to. I'd never even seen her in heels. She always maintained that they made her walk like a zombie. "I hope you don't mind that we're walking," I said.

"I figured we would."

"There's something I want to show you on the way to dinner."

She raised her eyebrows. "I don't know if I'm up for any surprises tonight, Connor."

"What are you up for?" I asked, walking around so I'd be on the street side of the sidewalk.

"Dinner."

"Just dinner?"

"Maybe dessert," she said.

"I'll see what I can do."

She tucked some hair behind her ear and strolled along next to me. "Is it weird to be back?"

"What do you mean?"

"I mean, living here again," she said. "After all this time."

I shrugged. "It's weird to be in my folks' house without them there."

"Have you been to their place in Florida?"

"Twice," I said. "It's in a development full of people their age."

"That's nice."

"Yeah. I suppose if my knees were shot and my skin were hanging off me, I wouldn't want to be living on the Miami strip either."

She laughed.

"What?"

"The thought of your folks on the Miami strip."

"Ridiculous, right?"

"First of all," she said. "Your dad would probably get arrested for wearing his pants so high."

"Probably."

"And I can't imagine how the clubbing crowd would react to your mom's collection of plaid handbags."

"I got her another one for Christmas."

"I love people who are easy to buy for," she said. "Like you know anything plaid will be cool with your mom, and you can always get Helly a crystal."

"Everyone should have a thing like that to make people's lives easier."

"What would yours be?" she asked.

I squinted up at a cottonwood tree as we walked under it. "I'm always happy with tennis balls."

"I suppose they're great for making friends with potential clients."

"Bingo," I said. "And you never turn down art supplies. I've never known you to at least."

She cast her eyes down and kicked some fluffy tufts of seed. "How does this place compare to Cali?"

"The winters are a joke there," I said. "At least where I was."

"Uh-huh."

"And there's this weird energy people have. Like everyone's in a big hurry, but they don't want you to know it."

"So they're not as chill as their reputation would lead you to believe?"

"No. Don't get me wrong. They're way chiller than people from the East Coast in terms of their default setting, but they're not quite as flighty and earthy as I thought they'd be."

She nodded.

"And what about you?" I asked. "Helly told me you've only been back a few days in years."

"Yeah. Just to check on her."

"Does small town life not suit you?"

She shrugged. "I think it does actually, but it scares me at the same time."

I furrowed my brow. "Why?"

"Because a place like Glastonbury can suck you in, ya know? Like mud."

"You like mud."

"I also like how easily mud washes off."

"So what are you saying? You think it's a nice place to visit, but you wouldn't want to live here?"

"No," she said. "It's not that. It's just… it's not really a singles hot spot, is it?"

"Are you kidding? You obviously haven't been to the new nightclub."

"There's a nightclub here?"

I shook my head. "No. Not unless you count the bingo club, but they do stay out pretty late on a Friday."

She rolled her eyes. "I was starting to think this place might've really changed."

"Not at all. I think the biggest change in the last few decades is the fact that Heatons started selling laptops, but otherwise it's probably not much different from when Helly first moved here."

"That's what I thought," she said, stepping over the sidewalk cracks.

"Personally, though, I think there's something nice about the fact that what you see is what you get."

And as I glanced at Laney out of the corner of my eye, I couldn't help but wish everything were so simple.

SEVENTEEN

- Laney -

I never used to wonder if I'd be in Glastonbury forever.

I did think I'd be with him, though, and that wherever we ended up would be perfect. As long as we were together.

So to say it was surreal to be walking along with him in such a familiar place- having such familiar feelings- would be an understatement.

Too bad about us being estranged... And all those wilderness years where we were lost to one another.

But I kept forgetting about all that, as if no time had passed at all. Or as if it had passed, but we hadn't left each other's side.

And I knew I shouldn't revel in the mystery of that feeling.

But it felt good.

Too bad the feeling was a lie. We hadn't stayed together. We hadn't been inseparable, and thanks to me, he spent some of that time feeling like shit.

And I felt bad, too.

But even if I'd had the wisdom to admit I'd made a mistake, I was too stubborn to do so. Besides, I'd convinced myself that he hated me after I turned down his proposal, and it's surprisingly easy to avoid people who hate you- even if it's all in your head.

Even if you still love them very much.

But he didn't seem bitter.

If anything, he seemed better than ever. And he wasn't treating me as hostilely as I deserved to be treated, which made the whole situation even harder.

It was the same problem we always had. Or rather, that I always had.

It's not like I expected him to treat me like my mother did, calling me nasty names that seemed to speak up at the back of my mind every time I did something good or had a fleeting moment of pride.

And I didn't expect him to treat me like her boyfriend did, spitting in my face as he yelled at me and pulling my hair as I sank down against the wall.

I knew that was wrong.

But Connor's behavior was on the other side of the spectrum. Sure, it was obviously the right side, the side where most people felt comfortable, but for me it just felt like another extreme.

And extremity frightened me.

It frightened me as a kid in an abusive household, and it frightened me as an adult. Even when the extreme feelings I had were good ones. Like love.

God I was terrified of the way I used to love Connor.

So when he asked if I could exist in that state forever, how could I say yes?

It seemed impossible.

I mean, I may have been attracted to color, but I felt safest in an all beige room.

I may have wigged out to the occasional dance track, but classical music made me feel like I was on solid ground.

I may have felt alive the few times I'd been skinny dipping, but I'd rather be cocooned in thick blankets any day.

And the love I felt for Connor back then was like skinny dipping in a hot pink lake that bubbled to the sound of the bass.

Of course, I didn't know how to articulate that then.

So I just said no and turned my back on the exciting feelings I couldn't trust.

And after having spent almost two years with Henry trying to become a person who could tolerate feeling safe and loved, I freaked out again.

Except deep down I knew it was different.

Because I wasn't afraid of the way I loved Henry the way I was afraid of my love for Connor.

And I didn't know what to make of that.

Did that mean it was bigger? More real? Less real?

I followed him through the gates of the park. I thought we were just taking the shortcut into downtown like we'd done a thousand times, but he stopped in the middle of the crumbling basketball court and hooked his thumbs in the pockets of his noticeably well-fitting jeans.

"So," he said, looking around.

"So," I echoed, my eyes scanning the park. The playground equipment looked more worn than I remembered and the old climbing wall was missing more than half its grip hooks.

"This is what I wanted to show you."

I tilted an ear towards him. "Did you think I'd be more or less surprised than I am?"

"This park's about to get a makeover."

"Thank god," I said. "So the surprise is more like a before and after reveal?"

He nodded.

"What's it got to do with me?"

"Nothing," he said. "Unless you want it to."

"I'm listening."

He sighed. "To make a long story short, the crumbling basketball court has somehow become my problem."

"Dave still getting you to do his dirty work?"

He smiled out of one side of his mouth. "Some things never change, huh?"

"Go on."

"But the court's not the only part of the park that could use a facelift."

"That's putting it kindly."

He nodded towards the climbing wall. "Apparently the climbing wall can't be reinstated because there's no life guard on duty here… to paraphrase some legislative bullshit."

"Because kids aren't as hardy as they used to be?"

"Exactly," he said. "But it's a perfectly good wall."

I cocked my head at it, letting my eyes scan the large bricks that made up the freestanding structure. "It's just ugly."

"I couldn't agree more," he said. "If you ask me, it needs a lick of paint."

I squinted at him. "Why are you looking at me like that?"

"Sorry, was that not obvious enough?" He cleared his throat. "Let me try again."

I raised my eyebrows.

"I said, if you ask me, it needs a lick of paint," he said, extending his outstretched arms towards the wall like he was Vanna White revealing an enormous vowel.

"Okaaay."

"Jesus, Laney. Are you just being dense because you like it when I act like an idiot?"

"Are you saying you think I should paint this wall?"

He squared up to me. "That's exactly what I'm suggesting."

"I can't paint this wall, Connor."

"Why not?" he asked.

"It's not my job for one thing."

"It's as much your job as anything else right now."

"That's rude," I said. "Besides, I haven't picked up a paintbrush in-"

"Too long," he said. "I know."

I shook my head.

"Just hear me out." He stepped up to me. "Close your eyes for a second."

"I don't want to."

"Do it."

I groaned and closed them.

"Remember the first big canvas you did? Remember how terrified you were of wrecking it?"

I opened my eyes. "This is stupid."

"Close your damn eyes."

"Fine."

"Remember how you overcame your anxiety and painted that awesome tree frog?"

I smiled. "It was an awesome tree frog, wasn't it?"

"It was. Do you remember how Helly put it up at the block party and you were famous for ten minutes?"

"I think it was more like fifteen," I said. "But yes."

"Remember that time we went to the beach and you sketched the lobster I ordered so we could remember its beauty forever?"

I kept my eyes squeezed shut. "I remember all the butter sauce that dripped down your chin while you ate that poor thing. Are we done?"

"One more memory," he said, his voice right behind my head.

I felt a charge travel up the back of my neck.

"Remember that field of wildflowers we used to play hide and seek in?" he asked, walking around me.

"I don't remember the sex ed teacher calling it hide and seek, but obviously I do."

"You know how you used to braid the wild grass together with the purple flowers to make little chains for your head and ankles?"

"Yeah." As if I could forget.

"You know I could go on, right?"

"I beg you not to," I said. "I'm getting hungry literally and also for your point."

"Open your eyes."

I opened them, and as I looked at his hopeful face, all the warm feelings I'd tried to forget about flooded my chest.

"You have a gift for making things beautiful, Laney."

"I don't know." I glanced at the wall behind him. "I wouldn't even know where to start."

"I know it won't be an easy job," he said. "But it's a job that will have been worth doing if it inspires even one little kid."

I folded my arms. "An unpaid job, I take it?"

"Will you do it?" he asked.

"As a favor to you?"

He shook his head. "No. Because you want to."

EIGHTEEN
- Connor -

"It's been way too long since I had fish and chips," Laney said, focusing on the paper bundle spread across her lap.

"I'm glad you still like it-"

"Like it?" she said, turning to me with a vinegar soaked French fry poised near her mouth. "It's a dream come true."

I laughed.

"I was so worried you were going to take me somewhere with silverware."

"I thought about it."

She shook her head and eyed her next bite of fish. "Cloth napkins are so overrated."

"Is that why you chose to work in the diner?"

She swallowed. "I chose to work in the diner because they were hiring and I could walk there from my apartment."

"What's your apartment like?"

"Do you remember the closet in the master bedroom at Jimmy Smolen's house?"

I nodded.

"It was like that, but with cockroaches and black mold instead of fur coats and designer handbags."

"Was?"

"I don't live there anymore."

I felt a burning sensation in my chest. "You live with Henry."

"I did," she said. "For a short while."

I crumpled the paper from my fish and chips and leaned back against the bench.

"Have you lived with anybody since-"

I raised my eyebrows.

"I last saw you?"

I nodded. "I had a few roommates in college, yeah."

"No," she said. "I mean a woman. Like one you were romantically involved with."

"Once."

"What was her name?" she asked.

"I don't really want to talk about it."

She licked her lips. "It would make me feel better."

"I'm sure it wouldn't."

"C'mon, Connor," she said, taking a sip of Sprite. "My life is a shambles right now. The least you could do is admit you've failed at something in the last few years."

"I didn't fail," I said. "The pregnancy did."

She lowered her soda. "What?"

I sighed. "She was a student in one of my classes."

"At vet school?"

I nodded. "We were seeing each other on and off for a while."

"And she got pregnant?"

"Yeah." I ran a hand through my hair. "So I asked her to move in with me."

Laney crumpled the paper wrapping around what was left of her dinner and stared at her lap.

"We lost the baby, though- a little girl- and decided to go our separate ways after that."

Laney looked at me through watery eyes.

I took a deep breath.

"You're right," she said. "I don't feel better."

I reached an arm over the back of the bench and stared at the manicured gardens in the middle of the square. "I'd appreciate if you kept that to yourself," I said. "It's not exactly common knowledge around here."

"Of course."

"It was an accident."

She raised her eyebrows.

"We were being careless."

She pursed her lips.

"I wouldn't have moved in with her and tried so hard to make it work if it hadn't been for the baby."

"I understand," she said. "And I'm so sorry."

"Life happens," I said. "At least I learned from it."

"What did you learn?" she asked, crossing a leg towards me.

"That I definitely want kids," I said. "Eventually. With the right person."

She squinted at me, her eyes searching my face.

"I couldn't believe how much I wanted that little girl," I said. And it was true. Losing her broke my heart for a second time. We were going to call her Sarah. Because it means princess, and I had every intention of spoiling her rotten.

"Do you guys keep in touch?"

I shook my head. "No. I think she married the guy she dated after me, but I'm not sure. It doesn't matter now. I didn't love her. I'm just glad she was able to move on after what we went through."

"And what about you?" she asked.

"What about me?"

"Are you okay?"

"Of course I'm okay, Laney. I got on with it. What choice did I have?"

She reached her hand for my bundled wad of trash and walked it to the garbage can across the paved path.

I watched the hem of her little blue dress and hoped sharing that with her hadn't been a mistake. "Do you have room for dessert?" I asked, rising off the bench.

"Maybe after a ramble," she said. "And thanks for dinner, by the way."

"You're welcome," I said. "I hope I didn't spoil it with my honesty at the end there."

She stopped walking and put a hand on my shoulder. "Of course not. I really appreciate you trusting me with that."

I felt a pinch in my chest. Didn't she know there was nothing I wouldn't trust her with? That there was a time when I trusted her with everything from my heart to my unborn children? No matter.

The important thing was that being around her was getting less painful by the minute, and that could only be a good thing for my heart and my head.

"So were you thinking Homer's milkshakes or frozen chocolate bananas at Eddie's?"

I shook my head. "Oh my god. I haven't had a chocolate dipped banana since I was a teenager."

"If we're lucky, they still do the one with the peanuts," she said, her eyes following an orange Frisbee on the other side of the park.

"I actually thought we'd swing by Dave's for dessert."

"Dave's?" She cocked her head at me. "Like Dave Dave?"

"Yeah. He's having a barbeque for some family thing. I imagine there'll be an entire selection of desserts there, including his wife's apple tarts which are good enough to die for."

"He's still with Amber?" she asked.

"He is. They've got three kids now. All girls."

"Wow."

"The oldest two are almighty terrors," I said. "But the youngest is still little enough that she just lays there and looks kind of spooked all the time."

She laughed, and the sound shattered the heavy cloak of sadness I felt I'd flung over us.

She scrunched her face. "I don't know if Dave would appreciate me rocking up to his house uninvited after all this time."

"Maybe not," I said. "But that's not a problem because you are invited."

"I am?"

"I talked to him about it earlier this week. Said you were in town and that you might come along."

"Was this before or after I said I'd have dinner with you?" she asked, her eyes pining mine to the back of my skull.

"Does it matter?"

"It was before, wasn't it?"

I nodded.

"You were that confident that I was going to say yes?" she asked, craning her neck forward. "Even when you knew I was seeing someone else?"

"No. To be honest, I had absolutely no confidence in you at all."

Her lips fell apart. "What's that supposed to mean?"

"That it's been years since I was in a position to guess what you might do."

"So what would make you ask him?" she asked. "When I'd been nothing but a jerk?"

I shrugged. "I guess I was just confident in my ability to keep asking."

NINETEEN
- Laney -

There were a thousand more questions I wanted to ask him. Like what stage of the pregnancy his ex was in when she lost the baby and whether or not they'd already bought a crib and little pink footie pajamas.

God that must've been heartbreaking.

And despite how selfish it was to think of myself in light of that news, I couldn't help but notice a shameful feeling bubbling up in me. Was it jealousy? Was I jealous that he had been that close to someone, that he'd shared something so intense with someone that wasn't me?

Obviously I used to think I'd be the one to experience that with him, that he would press his ear against my stomach and stuff pillows behind my back, that he would bring me ice cream in the night and bounce my children on his knee.

If I could even have kids, that is. Half the time I was sure I'd never be equipped to have a family, especially considering the bullshit parenting I was subjected to during my upbringing. I mean, I would literally have to do the opposite of everything my mom did.

And did the world really need my offspring? I just found out pineapples don't grow on trees two weeks ago. If I didn't even know stuff like that, how the hell did I think I was going to be able to answer the big questions?

Then again, kids could Google everything these days. Plus, you didn't really have to tell them the truth about anything until their ability to remember kicked in, and when was that- age five? Could I smarten up in that amount of time?

Whatever.

There was no chance Connor told me that so that I would dwell on the thought of him impregnating me for the rest of the night. He was just being honest.

Besides, it could've been me if I hadn't blown it, and things were messy enough without me going out of my way to stomp through the puddles of my own regret.

Worst of all, I felt some seedy smug feeling over his admission that he didn't love her. I mean, what the fuck was my problem? I broke up with him.

Had all those years I'd told myself that I wanted what was best for him been a lie?

Begrudging him any love he might have experienced over the years was downright cruel. Sometimes I swear I was the worst person on Earth.

We rounded the corner, and I noticed some brightly colored balloons hovering over a mailbox a few doors down.

"Is that their house?" I asked.

"Yeah."

"It's really nice," I said, wondering how the hell they could afford it.

"Amber's aunt left her some money when she died that covered the deposit."

I nodded. "I see."

"But the mortgage is still crushing Dave a little more each day so feel free to make a fuss about the place."

"Will do."

We followed the sound of screaming kids and muffled chatter up the driveway and around the stone house. When the backyard opened up, my jaw nearly dropped.

It was big enough that Amber had rented a bouncy castle for the day, and despite the fact that they already had one of those enormous trampolines, there was still plenty of room to spare.

Best of all, the large trees around the perimeter of the property were stunning.

I saw a hand shoot up by the grill and Connor waved back, his hand gracing my lower back as we headed towards Dave.

When we arrived at the grill beside the expansive stone patio, Dave closed it, hung the spatula on the handle, and stepped away from the heat.

"Well if it isn't Laney Price," he said, pressing his cheek to mine.

"Hi," I said. "It's nice to see you."

"How long are you going to be in town?" he asked, his tone strangely formal, as if I'd just walked into the middle of a police interview.

"I'm not sure," I said.

"What brings you back?" he asked.

I desperately wanted to mumble some bullshit about being in a transitional period, but it sounded so lame in my head I froze for a moment.

"She's got some loose ends to tie up," Connor interjected. "And she might extend her stay to paint a mural on the old climbing wall at York Street Park."

Dave raised his eyebrows. "No shit."

I shrugged.

"You must be doing really well to consider taking such a lengthy unpaid job," he said.

"And you must be doing really well to be living in this castle," I said, pissed at the air of judgement in his voice.

He clenched his jaw as he blushed.

"Congratulations on baby number three, by the way," I said. "Connor was just telling me that you've become quite the family man."

"Yeah," Dave said, wiping his hands on his Kiss the Cook apron. "The love of a good woman can ruin a person that way."

"Is Amber around?" I asked, looking over my shoulder. "It's been ages since I've seen her."

He scanned the yard and pointed towards a table at the edge of the garden. "She's parked next to the white wine over there," he said. "And I should warn you she hasn't moved from that spot all night so-"

"I'm going to pop over and say hi," I said, stealing a glance at Connor. "And leave you guys to it."

After Connor smiled and nodded at me, I headed to where Amber was sitting with another woman, who was rolling a small stroller back and forth beside her chair.

Amber stood up when she saw me coming and stomped her heels in the grass like she was dancing on hot coals. "Laney! Oh my god!"

"You look amazing," I said, pulling her into a hug.

"So do you!" she said. "It's so wonderful to see you."

"You too."

"Would you mind rolling this stroller while I run to the bathroom," the young mother who smelled like breastmilk asked. "I'd love to meet and greet you, but I'm actually bursting-"

"No problem," I said, reaching for the handle of the stroller.

"So," Amber said, draining her wine and pouring a glass for each of us. "What have you been up to? I was just thinking about you the other day."

"Oh?"

She nodded. "Some of the girls and I volunteered to paint the Glee Club float for the Fourth of July Parade, and halfway through our meeting- aka wine binge at Jeri's- we realized most of us can barely even draw a musical note freehand. Don't even get me started on the treble clef. Anyway, since you were always the best at art in high school, you popped into my head."

I smiled.

"And sometimes- and by sometimes I mean every other day- when my little girls play dress up and put wigs on, you cross my mind. They mostly have Disney princess wigs, but they don't have one that works for Pocahontas or Mulan yet."

"Thanks for thinking of me, Amber," I said, taking a sip of wine as I rolled the stroller gently in the grass. "That's really nice to hear."

"Are you kidding? I think about you all the time," she said, leaning forward and batting the lashes around her green eyes. "Well, maybe not as much as some people-" Her eyes strayed behind me, and I followed them over my shoulder to where Connor was still talking to Dave by the grill.

"I didn't realize Dave missed me that much," I said.

"Not Dave, silly."

I cocked my head.

"Oh, that was a joke." Amber tapped her long nails on the base of her wine glass. "I get it."

"Anyway, that's nice of you to say, but I'm pretty sure Connor's been preoccupied with plenty of other things."

She dropped her chin and kept her eyes on me. "Oh come on, Laney. Don't be naïve. You and I both know there are only two things that have ever preoccupied Connor."

I raised my eyebrows.

"And the other one's the animal kingdom."

TWENTY
- Connor -

Watching her from across the yard made me feel like a teenager again.

I was always so aware of her back then no matter what we were up to.

Even that first day I saw her sitting by herself in the cafeteria wearing geeky glasses that failed to hide how beautiful she was, I had to go over.

And I'd been like a moth to a flame ever since.

Frankly, by the time we graduated she was almost like a limb.

That's why her severing ties had been so shitty for me.

Because it didn't feel like I'd merely broken up with someone. It felt like part of me had been cut off and cast away.

And as I watched her bounce Elly Cartwright's new baby on her knee, I decided that it was wise to recall how hurt I'd been.

Because if I wasn't careful, it could happen again.

It was strange, though. Normally I was such a level headed guy. Anyone would've described me as a rational person. But the attraction I had to Laney made me stupid and vulnerable, and I could feel it in every cell of my body.

It was like one of those friendships where you know the other person means infinitely more to you than you do to them, but even imagining life without them is so much more painful than that realization that you make a conscious choice to take what you can get.

Because your life is richer with them in it.

Logically, I should've spent the evening flirting with the Detgens like a normal single guy who has his priorities straight.

Instead, I preferred to show Laney a good time. Just once more. Just in case it was my last chance.

And I could tell by the look on Dave's face that he didn't understand why I was doing this to myself.

"Did you have a nice time?" I asked as we strolled back the way we came, across the park and down the street with the fragrant cherry blossom trees.

Laney nodded. "It went better than I thought it would, actually."

I furrowed my brow. "How did you think it would go?"

"I don't know. I guess I was worried I wouldn't really fit in."

"Why would you feel that way?" I asked. "You must've known over half the people there."

She shrugged.

A firecracker went off in the distance.

She looked at me.

"Kids down by the lake," I said.

"Some things never change, eh?"

I smiled.

She took a deep breath. "I suppose I'm just so used to going to parties in New York where there's no pressure to fit in. On the contrary, everyone prides themselves on not fitting it, on the fact that they're different."

"Sure."

"But this is such a tight knit community," she said. "Not fitting in here can be isolating and scary."

"You looked like you felt comfortable."

"I did," she said. "I'm relieved how much actually. Amber especially went out of her way to make me feel welcome."

"Yeah, she's a sweetheart. And she was always fond of you."

"Which is more than I can say for Dave," she said, keeping her eyes on the sidewalk.

"Don't mind him. Being a good host doesn't come naturally to him."

"It's fine. I have a thick enough skin that I can handle it, but he was borderline interrogating me."

"What did you expect?" I asked.

"Sorry?"

"What did you expect?"

"I don't know," she said. "To not be interrogated at a barbeque?"

"I'm sure he has his reasons."

"And what might they be?" she asked.

I shrugged. "Who knows?"

Laney stopped in her tracks. "I bet you do."

"It doesn't matter. Come on."

"No. It does matter," she said. "He's worried I'm going to hurt you again, isn't he?"

"He's worried about a lot of things," I said, looking into her blue eyes.

"Don't put that on me, Connor."

I raised my eyebrows.

"I'm not the only adult in this relationship."

"What relationship, Laney?"

She cocked her hip. "Don't play stupid. You know this isn't normal- what we have. It isn't right."

I scratched the back of my head. "What's not right about it? We used to date, and I took you out as a gesture of goodwill."

"Why?" she asked, folding her arms.

"Because eating alone is overrated."

"But you should hate me," she said. "You shouldn't even be able to look at my face."

I waved her ridiculous comments away and headed down the street.

"Don't walk away," she said, hurrying after me. "You owe me an explanation."

I turned around at the bottom of Helly's driveway. "I don't owe you shit, Laney."

Her eyes grew wide.

"And you know it."

She swallowed.

"But I could never hate you, okay? Believe me, I've tried."

Her eyes bounced back and forth between mine.

"I loved you for too long." I set my hand on top of the low picket fence.

Her eyes started to water.

"And I can't forget," I said. "Even if I could I wouldn't want to-"

She stepped forward and kissed me then, pressing her soft lips to mine.

At first they felt foreign, but as soon as she parted them, my muscle memory and my emotional memory came to life.

And I kissed her back. How could I not? I did it as much out of the attraction I'd felt to her all night as I did out of curiosity.

And as I pulled her lower back towards me, all the bullshit melted away, all the stress, all the energy I'd put into fighting the fact that I still cared for her.

When she finally stepped back, I didn't know what to say.

Kissing her was even better than I remembered.

She didn't say another word, either. She just pursed her lips, walked around me, and headed up the driveway to Helly's house.

When she opened the front door, she looked back over her shoulder at me and then away again mid blush.

How she had the wherewithal to walk away was a mystery.

I took a few steps backwards and then headed up my own driveway, my lips still buzzing from the energy of her kiss.

My mind raced with questions about what came over her. Should I read into it? Did it mean something? Or did she just do it to shut me up or thank me or because she was unusually vulnerable right now with everything she was going through?

I didn't know. I couldn't know.

Because I'd fucked up.

I shouldn't have let her walk away. Not like that. Hell, I shouldn't have even let her come up for air.

After all, talking was doing nothing but getting us into trouble. But it hadn't crossed my mind that we could just skip that step. Just not talk. Just feel.

And why not? She'd said it herself- we were both adults.

So what if we wanted to pretend things were different for a few minutes. Was that really so bad? We weren't hurting anyone but ourselves.

As I unlocked the door and greeted Sarge, I couldn't help but think about the Choose Your Own Adventure Books, and how I wished I'd turned the pages differently just now.

Because even though it wasn't worth regretting the past, it was still the quality of my present days that mattered most.

And if the whole world ended tomorrow, I'd have to die knowing that I let her walk away.

Again.

TWENTY ONE
- Laney -

When I got home, Helly was asleep on the couch with an open book about gems on her chest. Meanwhile, an infomercial was making an aggressive offer on a steam mop in the background.

I wriggled the book from her arms, turned off the TV, and covered her with a blanket.

I knew better than to wake her up.

She took her dreams very seriously, and if you woke her while she was having one, she'd sulk the whole next day like you'd shredded her plane ticket to a far off land.

Which I could understand.

I'd been having crazy dreams lately myself, and while most of them were dreams I often wanted to wake up from- dreams about my mother or dreams where I'd wake up in a bed next to Henry's teeth in a glass- I, too, hated to be woken up during a good dream.

But I wasn't worried about dreaming that night.

Not only would I have been lucky to get any sleep at all, but if I went to sleep, I wouldn't be able to enjoy the reeling wonder I felt in my whole body as a result of kissing Connor again.

But while it was magical to feel so overwhelmingly home again in all the best ways, I shouldn't have done it.

I mean, what the hell was I thinking?

Of course, I knew the answer to that question- I wasn't. I wasn't thinking at all.

I just- I don't know… When he said he didn't hate me, that he couldn't forget about loving me, and that he didn't even want to, I just had to kiss him.

It's not that I didn't believe his words, but I wanted to feel them.

And I wanted to answer them.

And I knew if I tried to speak I'd just make a big mess of one of the most generous, kind moments I'd enjoyed in quite some time.

But I had to apologize.

It was too late to say I was sorry for breaking his heart, for ending things the way I did, and for not having the decency back then to try and explain.

But I could at least apologize for crossing the line at the end of the driveway. After all, he didn't deserve for me to show up and turn his life on its head when he'd done such a good job moving on.

So as I lied awake in bed that night, I apologized over and over, trying to get it right, trying to sound sincere.

Which was desperately difficult because deep down, I wasn't genuinely sorry.

I was happy I kissed him. Elated even. Intoxicated.

But that didn't make it okay.

And I didn't want him to think I was crazy.

Everyone else could. That was fine. But not him.

***

I remembered the kiss before I even opened my eyes.

It was the last thing I thought about the night before and the first thing that popped into my head that morning.

And I knew the longer I put off apologizing the worse it was going to be.

I sat up and stretched my arms over my head, my eyes adjusting to the light as they located the Minnie Mouse clock on my bookshelf.

It was nine o'clock.

I didn't hear anyone else up in the house, which was odd as Helly usually sang to herself in the mornings, especially on the weekend after some good dreams.

But when I went to the window, I saw her in the backyard, rolling tires around in an effort to create a new plot of flower beds. She'd mentioned earlier that week that she was keen to create a rainbow effect against the left wall and insisted it would look better than it sounded.

I knew I should go out and greet her, but I was in a hurry to put my immature behavior behind me so I brushed my teeth, made sure I didn't have a nest of hair bunched anywhere on my head, and washed my face.

I couldn't stop myself from putting on a smidge of blush, but I dismissed the rest. Putting a full face of makeup on for my apology seemed to cheapen it somehow.

Then I snuck out the front door and tried to control my breathing as I headed up the path to his house.

I rang the bell and listened to the tweeting birds while I waited.

"Laney," he said when he saw me. He was in a white t-shirt and pajama pants, but it didn't look like I'd woken him up.

"Can I talk to you?"

He stepped back so I could come in.

I stayed by the front door while he closed it. He smelled like a sleeping man, and being so close to his pheromones gave me goosebumps.

"What's up?" he asked, his dark eyes searching mine.

"I came to apologize."

He furrowed his brow.

"I shouldn't have kissed you last night. I don't know what got into m-"

He grabbed my face and kissed me, inhaling the bullshit excuses that had been on the tip of my tongue.

My back bowed as he pulled me to him and ran his fingers through my hair, clenching a clump of my bedhead in his fist.

In that moment I wished he would kiss me forever and that I would never have to make sense of my feelings.

He pulled my shirt off over my head and his lips found mine again like a magnet while he unhooked my t-shirt bra with one hand.

I felt him swell against me and my breath hitched in my throat.

"Damnit, Laney," he said, almost growling as he walked forwards and lowered me down against the staircase. He dropped his head to my neck and his stubble tickled me, causing a hot shiver to vibrate up my spine.

I grabbed the sleeves of his shirt as he dropped his hands to my chest, followed by his mouth.

When he pulled my leggings down, I felt the carpeted stairs on my ass and slid my fingers into his thick hair, letting my head fall back onto the step behind it.

He pushed my legs apart and licked my slit, causing my whole body to gush towards him.

My ankles were still stuck in my leggings, but he lifted them over his head so they hung down his back and brought his face between my thighs again.

I reached for the banister with one hand and gripped the stairs with the other as he licked me, scooping me out with an intensity I never could have prepared myself for.

I moaned and bucked against his face.

He put his hands around my waist, lapping at me harder all the time.

"Oh god, Connor," I whispered. "That feels too good."

He stuck his fingers inside me and stretched me open.

I cried out and arched my back.

He crawled forwards so his face was over mine and my tied ankles stayed wrapped around him.

I panted through parted lips.

He didn't say anything. He just watched my eyes while he finger fucked me.

"You're going to make me come," I said, staring at his mouth through half closed eyes.

He forced his fingers deeper and kissed me, churning my insides and my tongue at the same time until I felt completely vulnerable and totally out of control.

Then he lifted me and carried me up the stairs to the landing.

When he laid me back down, he raised up onto his knees, forcing my leggings to spring from one of my ankles so I was no longer bound.

He was breathing hard as he pulled his shirt off, and the sight of his abs made me wilt inside.

It was as if they'd multiplied since the last time I saw them, and now the chiseled cuts in his stomach where too many to count.

Then he pulled his pants down, his eyes on me as his dick sprang from his pajama pants.

He stroked it over me and looked me up and down, his eyes falling from my lips to my tits.

"Connor, I-"

"Shut up," he said, his face serious. "I'm sick of your shit." He held himself over me, his hands planted on both sides of my head. "It's my fucking turn to make a point," he said, reaching down and guiding the tip of his dick inside me.

I furrowed my brow as he pushed his way in.

Then he dropped to his elbows, sucked the delicate skin of my neck, and buried himself inside me.

TWENTY TWO

- Connor -

"You're so big," she breathed.

The sound of her voice made my mouth water. Of course, I'd always been big. She just had no point of comparison back then so she probably took me for granted.

But like I said, I was sick of her shit. I was sick of her making excuses and acting like she didn't deserve to feel good, to feel loved, to be the center of attention.

And I'd laid awake all night regretting the fact that I'd let her walk away.

I sure as hell wasn't going to listen to her apologize, especially when I knew she wasn't sorry.

The face she made last night before she went inside wasn't the face of a regretful person. It was the face of someone who was leaving against their will.

And if she didn't know her own mind well enough to know that it was a good thing she kissed me, then I obviously hadn't kissed her hard enough.

She dragged a hand down my chest, and I raised my face to look at her.

"You feel so good," she said, her crystal eyes bouncing back and forth between mine.

I clenched my jaw and drove into her, relishing how tight and wet she was as I savored her sweetness on my lips.

She tasted better than I remembered, better than any pussy I'd eaten in years.

I leaned up and lifted her hips into my lap so she could watch me fuck her, my swollen dick straining as I slid in and out of her.

Then I moved a hand to work her clit.

I wanted to make her come so hard she'd cry. Lord knows it wouldn't be the first time.

She reached her hands over her head, hiding her furrowed brows in one of her elbows.

"How's that?" I asked, her clit swelling for me. "Are you sorry about this, too? Are you sorry about how hard you're going to come on my dick?"

She shook her head.

"That's what I thought," I said, dropping her legs to my sides and sliding my hands under her back.

She moved like a rag doll as I rolled back at the top of the steps until she was straddling me.

"Now apologize with your pussy," I said, smacking her ass.

She fell forward so her face was just inches from mine.

I grabbed her ass in my hands and rocked her up and down my dick, crushing her clit against the base of my shaft between every thrust

She reached out to steady herself, placing her hands on both sides of my face so her tits swung over me.

I grabbed her face with one hand. "Come for me, Laney. Coat my dick like you used to."

She kept her eyes on me and licked her plump lips.

"That's it," I said, watching her face as I felt her pussy start to shudder. "Give it to me."

She started grinding against me like my body remembered, her weight all the way down on my cock.

"I'm coming," she said, letting out a moan that was music to my ears.

When she began to spasm, I rolled us onto our sides, fucking her clenching pussy with all the energy my hips could muster.

She kept her eyes on me as she jerked in my arms, spilling over my dick as I burst inside her.

"Fuck," she breathed, blinking her heavy eyelids at me.

"Fuck is right," I said, trying to catch my breath as her pulsing pussy milked my dick.

"You were incredible," she said.

"I always thought you brought that out in me," I said, pulling out of her and rolling onto my back.

"Was it something I said?" she asked.

I rolled my head towards her.

"In case I want to say it again."

One side of my mouth curled up, and I let my eyes trace the curves of her breasts and hips as she lay on her side.

"I don't really know what to make of what we just-"

"Just shut up," I said, suddenly conscious of a carpet burn sensation in my knees.

"You can't really get away with that afterwards, ya know?"

I raised my eyebrows. "Not everything needs to be analyzed, Laney."

"You think talking about this will ruin it?"

"I think talking about this will be a huge waste of your breath because there's no blood in my brain right now."

"Oh. Right."

"Though I do want to know what the hell you think you're doing showing up like that."

"Like what?"

"With bedroom eyes in a come fuck me t-shirt."

She laughed. "I was deliberately trying to look like shit, actually."

"What?"

"So my apology would seem more sincere."

I laughed.

"What's so funny?"

"I don't know where to start."

She raised her eyebrows. "Start with why you're fucking laughing at me."

I sighed. "First of all, you did a shitty job looking like crap."

She pursed her lips.

"And second of all, that was the least sincere, most bullshit apology I've ever heard in my entire life."

"Well you didn't exactly let me finish."

"I didn't have to," I said. "It was bullshit through and through."

"It wasn't bullsh-"

"Look, Laney. You don't have to be honest with me about everything," I said. "I get that that was a privilege I enjoyed when we were together back in the day. But the least you could do is not go out of your way to lie to me."

She swallowed.

"Which is exactly what you just tried to do."

The corner of her mouth twitched. "Before you so gallantly stopped me from making an ass of myself?"

"Extreme circumstances call for extreme measures."

Her cheeks were still bright pink. "Those were some pretty extreme measures all right."

"You're welcome."

She laughed. "How selfless of you."

"What can I say?" I leaned up to rest on my elbows. "I'm a selfless guy like that."

"You always were."

"No kidding," I said. "God knows that's not the first time I've had to fuck you to shut you up."

"How can you tell if I'm genuinely annoying or just being annoying because I want sex?"

"It's not in my interest to know the difference."

"Mmm." She sat up and looked around. "So now what?"

I reached for my pants. "I suppose I should give you the rest of the tour since you haven't seen the upstairs yet."

"Sounds good," she said, rising to her feet. "And in case I forget to mention it, I absolutely love what you've done with the landing."

FLASHBACK
- Connor -

Laney pulled some bread from the end of her sandwich and threw it down by Waddles where she was poking around the water's edge.

I crumpled the wrapper from my own sub and stuffed it in the outside pocket of my backpack.

"Do you think Waddles speaks duck?" she asked, her eyes on the speckled brown bird.

"Hard to say," I said, leaning back on the blanket and wriggling my back to get comfortable on the pebbly ground beside the lake.

"I like to think she does," Laney said. "I like to think the wild ducks are always inviting her to come hang out and she's like, 'naw, maybe later.'"

"And what if she means it?"

"You mean what if she takes off with a bunch of ducks someday?" she asked. "Or if she finds a handsome mallard who she thinks she'd be happier with?"

"Yeah." I pulled my sunglasses from where they were hanging in the front of my shirt and slipped them on so I could look at her without being bothered by the glare off the lake.

"I guess I'd have to be happy for her," she said, throwing another piece of bread. "I mean, she is a wild animal."

I laughed. "I don't know how wild she is. Wasn't she watching TV with Helly when I brought you home yesterday?"

Laney shrugged. "I don't think that makes her domesticated. I think that just means she's lazy."

I watched Laney pop the last bite of her sandwich in her mouth. She was wearing a baggy tank top and shorts that were so short the pockets poked out the front.

"We should probably head back," she said. "I haven't done any of my homework yet, and math always takes me six times longer than I think it's going to."

"It's not because you're stupid, ya know?" I said, sitting up and putting our picnic snacks back in my bag. "It's because you stop in the middle to do your nails and call Amber and watch American Idol."

"Not true."

"If you say so," I said. "But I bet if you did your math homework at my house while I did mine, you'd get it done in at least half the time."

"As if I could trust you to not distract me."

I pulled her close and she straddled my lap, twirling her fingers through my messy pile of blond hair.

"I suppose you're right," I said, kissing her. "But I'd leave you alone for at least a few minutes because you're so cute when you concentrate."

"I am not."

"You are."

Waddles splashed in the shallow water, and we both looked in her direction.

"What's that?" I asked, pointing near a piece of drift wood on the sandy bank.

Laney craned her neck in that direction and stood up. "I don't know." She kicked her flip flops over, slipped them on, and walked over to the item in question.

I watched her crouch down and dig around it.

"It's a bottle," she said.

"No kidding."

She squinted at me.

I craned my neck back. "What?"

"There's a message in it."

"What are the chances?" I asked, feigning surprise as best I could.

"Pretty slim since I can see all around the lake from here," she said, pulling it out of the sand with two hands. "So I doubt it's from a shipwreck."

"Can you tell what the message says?"

"Something tells me you can," she said, cocking her head. "Even from so far away."

Fuck. Why did she have to be such a smartass? I stood up and walked over.

"I can't get the cork out," she said, pulling it with her fingers.

"It must've been buried there a long time."

She made a skeptical face and handed it to me.

I pretended it was more difficult to open than it was before finally twisting the cork out of the clear glass bottle.

She tipped it over and reached a small finger inside to try and snag the note.

"This is so exciting," I said.

"I hope it's a map to buried treasure," she said. "Then I won't have to go home and do my homework."

She wiggled it out, dropped the bottle, and unrolled the homemade scroll.

I watched her mouth curl into a smile as her eyes scanned my invitation to prom.

"If only I knew who left it here," she said. "So I could give them my answer."

I groaned and rolled my eyes.

"Just kidding, babe," she said, draping her arms over my shoulders and pressing her lithe frame against me. "Of course I'll go to prom with you."

"Well that's a relief," I said, giving her a kiss. "For a second there I thought I'd have to rebury the damn thing and hope someone else came along."

"Good one."

I shrugged. "I try."

"We should celebrate."

"What did you have in mind?" I asked, slipping my hands under her shirt.

"Hmm." She looked around. "I've always wondered what was on the other side of that bush over there."

"That's so funny," I said, lifting her up. "So have I."

She wrapped her legs around my waist and held on tight as I walked into the tall grass and laid her down.

And if I wasn't already delighted she'd said yes, I certainly was ten minutes later.

TWENTY THREE
- Laney -

I felt giddy and smitten, and that was completely inappropriate considering the fact that I was a homeless person who was supposed to be recovering from a breakup and looking for gainful employment.

Instead, I was indulging in nostalgia by poking around Connor's room after having cheeky sex in his parents' house in a spot we'd never done it before.

It was surreal.

"I can't believe you still have them all," I said, running my fingers along the spines of the Choose Your Own Adventure Books.

"Why wouldn't I?" he asked from where he was sitting on the end of his bed.

I shrugged. "I don't know."

"My parents always threatened that they were going to get rid of my stuff, but I guess it was never a priority."

My eyes dropped to the next shelf where a row of cheap little league trophies stood in a row. "Most Improved?" I asked, holding one up.

"They got sick of giving me MVP."

"Wow," I said, setting the trophy back down. "That couldn't have made you popular with the other kids."

"The kids were fine with it," he said, leaning back on straight arms. "It was the parents who took issue."

I walked over to his desk. It looked smaller than I remembered, but the ticket stubs I'd paper clipped to the lampshade were untouched. "I forgot we saw some of these movies."

"Some of them were forgettable."

I looked over my shoulder at him. "The vodka we used to sneak in probably didn't help."

"It helped us find the comedy in movies that weren't supposed to be funny, though."

"It's a miracle we only got kicked out twice," I said. "By that old usher guy- what was his name? Something with an S."

Connor nodded. "I forgot about him. God he used to say the craziest shit to us."

I laughed. "I think he had some kind of Tourette's."

"He'd never get away with talking to kids like that now. Kids are too precious these days."

I turned around. "I don't understand how they're supposed to grow a thick skin if they're not allowed to rock climb over pavement and get cussed at by strangers."

"They're not. They're supposed to get coddled forever."

I shook my head. "But that's how you end up with college students saying they don't want to be graded anymore because it puts them under too much stress."

"I know," he said. "It's ridiculous. We've created an entire generation that can't cope with feedback."

I leaned against the desk. "I suppose we were lucky in some ways."

"No shit. I asked Dave the other day if he'd ever spanked any of his kids, and he laughed until he cried."

"Because it's so out of the question?"

"Yeah," he said. "Now don't get me wrong. I'm not all for corporal punishment or anything, but I got spanked and I turned out okay."

I craned my neck forward. "You got spanked?"

He nodded. "Twice"

"For what?"

"Once for kicking my babysitter in the shin."

I raised my eyebrows.

"I had my cleats on, and she said something mean about Dave's older sister and he just stood there."

"And the other time?" I asked.

"I put firecrackers in my teacher's mailbox."

I furrowed my brows. "What?"

"It's not like he was anywhere near it when I set them off."

"So how'd you get caught?"

He laughed. "He was watching from the window. Saw the whole thing. My dad knew before I even got home."

"Shit." Connor knew better than to ask if I got spanked. He knew more about my childhood than even Helly, though I'd told her a lot about it over the years. Still, I would've traded some spanks for the verbal abuse I got at that age in a heartbeat. "Is that where you learned it then?"

"What?" he asked.

"The spanking?"

He leaned an ear towards me. "What are you talking about?"

I folded my arms. "I'm talking about the one you gave me twenty minutes ago."

His face turned red. "I can honestly say that had nothing to do with my dad- or my childhood- and everything to do with the fact that I was so excited to see your ass after all these years I didn't know what to do with myself."

"Well, like you, I certainly learned my lesson."

"Good," he said. "Because I won't hesitate to smack that ass again if I need to."

It was my turn to look at the ground and blush.

"Speaking of which, is your back okay?" he asked.

"My back? Yeah, why?"

"Because I think I might have sustained some minor carpet burns on my knees," he said, reaching forward and covering them with his hands.

I laughed. "That'll teach you to fuck on the landing."

He shrugged. "It hadn't been christened yet. Besides, I didn't know whether I should turn towards this room, where we used to always hang out-"

My eyes swept the ceiling. I could've drawn this room from memory and gotten everything in its rightful place.

"Or my parent's room, but being with you made me forget that it was mine now."

"Sorry."

"Don't be," he said. "As long as you're okay."

"I'm fine," I said. "Way finer than I should be considering the circumstances anyway."

"Well, that's all most of us can hope for, isn't it?"

The doorbell rang a moment later, and Sarge came bounding out of the room down the hall and thumped down the steps.

"Where's he been?" I asked.

"Sleeping," he said. "He likes a little nap after his first feed of the day."

"Who doesn't?" I asked. "You expecting someone?"

He shook his head. "Nope."

I followed him downstairs and watched him toss a tennis ball towards the back of the house before opening the door.

"Helly," Connor said. "Hi."

Helly looked from Connor to me to Connor to me. "Laney. I thought you were still sleeping."

I descended the rest of the stairs. "I just popped over this morning to tell Connor... that I remembered something I forgot."

She narrowed her eyes at me. "Your shirt's on inside out."

"Oops," I said, wanting to disappear. "What's up?"

"I've been working quietly in the garden so I wouldn't wake my precious granddaughter." She shot me a look. "And I've just found some newborn kittens behind the shed."

Connor raised his eyebrows.

"They look healthy enough to me," she said, turning to Connor. "But I thought maybe you could give them a once over in case any of them needs anything their mother can't give them."

"I'd be happy to check them out," Connor said. "Give me a few minutes to let the dog out and grab my stuff, and I'll be right over."

"Thanks so much," she said. "And sorry to bother you."

"It's no bother, Helly," he said. "I'm glad you asked."

"Okay then. I'll see you shortly," she said, stepping back off the stoop. "And it's probably a good idea if Laney stays here," she said, failing to suppress a smile. "You know, so you don't get lost on the way."

TWENTY FOUR
- Connor -

"She's on to you," I said after I closed the door.

"Is what just happened written all over my face?" Laney asked, pulling her shirt off and turning it inside out.

I grabbed her and pulled her to me. "Are you sure you want to put that back on?" I asked, pressing her back against the banister. "I could make it worth your while to keep it off."

Her chest rose and fell in front of me, and I felt her nipples pucker through the thin fabric of her bra.

"I'm sure you could," she said. "But didn't you take some kind of oath?"

"I did, yeah, but I can't seem to remember why at the minute."

"Quit while you're ahead," she said, pushing me away.

I stepped back, a sly smile still on my face. "That must be the shittiest advice ever invented."

"Unless you're gambling," she said, pulling her shirt on the right way. "Then it's great advice."

I headed towards the back door where Sarge was chewing a rawhide bone. "When was the last time you gambled?" I asked, opening the door to let him out.

"I gambled on going out with you last night," she said, walking towards me in bare feet.

Seeing her in my kitchen with her blonde bed head framing her blue eyes made me feel too much. It hurt bad enough the other day, but now that I'd had her again- now that I knew she was sweeter and sexier than ever- it hurt even more.

Why did she have such a hold on me? After all the women I'd been with, why was she was still the one who made me want more, crave more, need more.

"That wasn't really a gamble, though," I said, pulling my house call bag out of a closet by the back door and setting it on the counter. "You knew we'd have a good time."

"No I didn't," she said. "It could've been totally awkward and painful."

"Painful?" I opened the bag and sifted through it with my fingers to make sure I had everything I might need to examine the kittens.

"You could've dug stuff up and thrown it in my face."

I lifted my eyes to her. "Like what? The fact that you broke my heart? That would've made for a shitty night out."

"I would've deserved it though."

"I disagree," I said. "Besides, you already know that, and I'm not sure what you've been telling yourself over the years, but most of our memories are good ones."

"I know," she said, lowering her voice. "Trust me, I know."

"Plus," I said, closing the bag. "I care about you, and the last thing you need right now is me piling on when you can't change the past anyway."

"Right."

"Regret is pain relived," I said. "Not pain relieved."

"So true."

"And you might have regrets, Laney, but I don't." I turned to look out the picture window behind me. Sarge was sniffing along the back fence, his tail wagging like it was hooked up to a motor.

"You don't have any regrets?" she asked.

"Not about what happened with us," I said. If anything, I was proud of how I handled myself. It would've been regrettable if I'd left without telling her how I felt, but I'd laid it all on the table.

I figured nothing good could come from hiding my feelings away. Love always seemed to me like the kind of thing that needed fresh air, the kind of thing you should give away every chance you get.

As far as I was concerned, that was the only way to live if you ever wanted it to come back to you.

And perhaps the fact that I'd given so much love to Laney all those years ago was why she'd crossed my path again. There was no way of knowing.

Regardless, part of me really wanted to ask if she had any regrets about us, about the way she handled it, about the blow she dealt that changed the course of our lives.

But I said I didn't have regrets. I never said I didn't have denial.

And if she was happy with her actions, I sure as fuck didn't want to hear about it.

I just wanted to see her smile, make her laugh, and if luck was on my side, make her come again.

Because that brief encounter was like reliving all the best nights of my life at once, and I was desperate for my next high.

A few minutes later, I called Sarge inside, gave him his bone back, and headed over to Helly's with Laney.

"Oh there you are," she said when she saw us. "I was beginning to worry Laney might have started remembering and forgetting again, and it would've taken you another half hour to make it over."

Laney gave Helly a hug and spoke softly in her ear. "You're hilarious, you know that?"

Helly craned her neck back. "There's nothing hilarious about me, young lady. You're the one who's so silly you need the boy next door to help you get dressed."

"Like you've never accidentally put a shirt on inside out," Laney said.

"Of course I have," Helly said. "Which is why I don't appreciate being bullshitted."

"So where are these kittens?" I asked.

"Behind the shed there," Helly said, pointing before turning back to Laney. "All I'm saying is that if you want to sleep out, at least have the decency to let me know so I don't worry."

"I didn't sleep out," Laney said. "I went over this morning. Connor-"

I turned to look over my shoulder.

"Tell Helly I only stopped by this morning."

"It's true," he said. "She only came by this morning, and I can assure you she did absolutely no sleeping at all."

Laney groaned.

"That's what I thought," Helly said, looking back at her. "No sleeping at all."

"I don't have to explain myself to you," Laney said. "I don't have to tell you when I wake up and if I need to go to the bathroom in the night and what time I'll be home."

"No," Helly said. "Of course you don't. But as a guest in my home, it sure would be thoughtful of you to say good morning when you wake up instead of sneaking around like a sixteen year old girl."

I knelt down by the kittens, afraid that if I looked back, I might get called out for my crooked grin.

"I trust you at least went to the door instead of climbing in through the window like you used to?" Helly asked.

"Of course I used the door," Laney said. "And why do you even know about the window thing?"

Helly laughed. "Because I wasn't born yesterday, honey, as you well know."

"I'm sorry," Laney said. "I should've said good morning."

"Thank you," Helly said. "Apology accepted. And I shouldn't have teased you for your early morning booty call, but I felt it was within my rights."

I glanced over my shoulder and saw that Laney had her red face in her hands. Then I turned back to the kittens, picking them up and checking their eyes and ears.

"How are they?" Helly asked.

"They look healthy," I said. "Except for this little grey one."

"What's the problem?" Laney asked, crossing her arms.

I looked over my shoulder. "She's blind."

TWENTY FIVE
- Laney -

Amber looked straight out of a fifties sitcom as she approached my outdoor table at Mimi's Café.

"I hope you weren't waiting long," she said, pulling out her chair. "I thought I'd just drop the kids off and, well, you know how mothers are-"

She flinched despite the fact that I smiled politely.

"Anyway, how are things?" she asked. "I can't even tell you how much I've been looking forward to this."

"Me too," I said, pouring some ice water into her glass.

"We should make this a regular thing."

"We should," I said, leaning back in my chair.

"That was your cue to tell me you're staying in Glastonbury forever because you can't bear the thought of missing one of my parties."

I raised my eyebrows. "To be fair, your Fourth of July party should've been in the pages of House and Garden Magazine."

She clasped her hands in front of her. "You are so sweet to say that."

"Any joy with the lawn?"

She shook her head. "It still looks like a flag. Dave is furious. I thought the paint would wash away at the first rain, but it's holding strong."

"Well, between you and me, staying has crossed my mind, but I don't think Helly can take living with Neo much longer."

"Neo?"

"The blind kitten we found behind the shed."

She furrowed her thinly manicured brows. "You called it Neo?"

"Yeah, like in the Matrix."

"I know. Dave loves that movie," she said. "But isn't Neo supposed to be, like, The One who brings peace?"

"Yup."

Her eyes grew wide. "That's a lot of pressure to put on a kitten."

I smiled. "I know, and he's totally not rising to the challenge. He is, however, the one who brings hilarity."

She raised her eyebrows.

"I mean, I know I shouldn't laugh at him because he's disabled, but he's genuinely good for at least one solid belly laugh a day."

Her smile dropped. "Please don't tell my daughters that. A kitten is just about the only thing they haven't realized they want yet."

"Sure."

"And I thought Helly loved cats?"

I shrugged. "She likes cats outside."

Amber cocked her head. "And she can't make an exception for a little blind cat?"

"She has been," I said. "But it's not fair to ask her to do that much longer. Plus, she's got so many crystals and jewel bellied trolls and wicker statues around that it's hard on Neo. He has trouble navigating around all her crap."

"Ahh. I can see how that would be tough for him," she said. "And as far as Helly, her reluctance to have cats inside contradicts the fact that I've always been positive she's a witch."

I laughed. "I'm sure she was in one of her lives, but she's not practicing now as far as I know."

Amber made a face like she was carefully processing the information.

"Oh before I forget," I said, reaching into my bag. "I brought you something for the girls."

"You didn't have to do that," she said. "It's bad enough that Dave and I spoil them rotten."

"Pocahontas," I said, holding up one wig. "And Mulan," I said, lifting the other.

Amber's face lit up.

"They're second hand," I said. "But I figured they wouldn't mind."

"Of course they won't," she said, taking them from me. "If anything, they'll start worshipping you so much they'll need a Laney wig next."

"You don't have to say they're from me-"

"What? Of course I do! They already think you're a celebrity."

I furrowed my brows. "Excuse me?"

"We've been going down to check out your mural at least twice a week. They're so excited about what you've done so far."

"Really?"

She nodded. "Well, not Suzie, cause she doesn't get excited about anything besides ear infections these days, but-"

"I'm sorry to hear that."

"It's fine," she said, raising her red nails towards the sky. "Or at least, I spend so much time thinking about it, I'd rather not talk about it now."

A teenage waiter brought some bread to the table, and we ordered two Waldorf salads and an order of fries to share.

"You know what I really want to talk about?" she asked.

I took a piece of soft French bread and tore it in half. "What?"

"How things are going with Connor."

I felt the blood rush to my cheeks.

"Ha! I knew it. You guys are so sprung."

I squinted. "Maybe not sprung."

"Yes, sprung. Totally. I've been telling Dave this would happen. You've been soulmates all along."

I lifted a hand between us. "Wait a second. You've been telling Dave what would happen?"

"That you guys would pick up right where you left off."

I swallowed.

"But he didn't believe me," she said. "He thinks you hurt Connor too bad for anything to happen."

I pursed my lips.

She reached for her water. "But it's all happened anyway, hasn't it?"

"Dave doesn't approve, does he?"

She swatted my concern from the air. "Dave's just worried about his friend."

"And you?"

She crunched an ice cube and set her glass down. "I think Connor can handle himself."

I nodded.

"And I think you're too smart to make the same mistake again."

"What mistake?" I asked.

"The mistake of taking him for granted when he's literally, like, the most eligible bachelor ever."

"Mmm."

She craned her neck forward. "You wouldn't hurt him again, would you?"

"I never meant to hurt him in the first place."

"That's irrelevant," she said. "What I'm trying to say is that, while it's obvious you guys are good together, he's ready for something serious, and if you can't be that, you shouldn't lead him on."

"I'm not leading him on. I'm just trying to figure out what I want."

"Sure."

I leaned back in the metal chair. "Besides, he told me he doesn't regret how things ended with us."

"Please tell me you don't believe that."

"Why shouldn't I? He said it to my face."

She shook her head and poured some olive oil into a shallow dish. "Maybe he doesn't regret that he proposed, but I'm sure he regrets that you said no."

I stuffed some bread in my mouth.

"Not that you can really regret other people's actions," she said. "Because that could make a man crazy-"

"You seem really sure about this."

She shrugged. "He and Dave have been best friends since there were firetrucks on their underwear."

"Right."

"Don't make that face," she said. "The past doesn't matter now. You're getting a second chance to realize how good you are together."

"And I'm taking it."

"I know you are," she said. "And I just want you to know I approve. I mean, I know you can't be in another person's relationship, but you guys were sickly sweet at our party on the Fourth."

"It's like no time has passed. It's kind of crazy."

"Crazy good?" she asked.

"I just don't want to get ahead of myself."

She narrowed her bright green eyes on me. "What do you mean?"

"Just between us-"

She nodded.

"I'm not convinced I deserve his forgiveness even if he's already given it to me."

"He has," she said. "And no offense, but I don't think that's what you should be worried about."

I furrowed my brow. "What should I be worried about?"

"Figuring out how to forgive yourself."

TWENTY SIX

- Connor -

The afternoon sun was rising higher in the sky, but the heavy heat was doing little to suppress my growing appetite.

I grabbed the shirt that was hanging over my shoulder and mopped my brow.

Fortunately, I was protected from the sun by the asphalt compactor's roof, but Laney was working away on the mural without shelter, her hair so blonde in the sun it was nearly blinding.

She was probably only a day or two from finishing, and while I knew she'd do a good job, I never could've imagined the colorful scene that would pour out of her. Wild animals decorated in psychedelic patterns were playing everything from hop scotch to double dutch, and I'd nearly flattened the basketball hoop twice getting lost in what she'd done.

It was beautiful. Almost as beautiful as she was.

And things were going well.

Yes, I'd fallen for her again, but I don't think that was the whole story.

To be honest, I think I never really got up after the first time I fell, and it was like no time had passed.

In the last few weeks, we'd picnicked by the lake, snuck vodka into the movie theatre, and revisited some of our favorite Choose Your Own Adventure Books. I'd shown her my office, fucked her in every bed in my house, and invited her to join me for countless walks with Sarge.

It was the happiest I'd ever been.

And she seemed happy, too, which made my chest swell with pride.

Of course, we hadn't had many serious talks, especially about our history. She'd tried to broach the subject, but I stopped her every time.

I didn't want to dissect the past. I wanted to live for the future, and I couldn't help but feel that overanalyzing our relationship is what spoiled it for us the first time around.

After all, when she wasn't second guessing herself, she was light and free and confident. She acted on her intuition, and the words that came out of her mouth made sense.

It was only when she started thinking about the decisions she'd cut herself off from and comparing herself to others that she got lost in a messy corner of her head.

But with every day we spent together, I became more aware of the fact that we hadn't committed to anything and that all our jovial fun could end in a second.

And I wanted more from her. Needed more. Deserved more.

Because the love I was prepared to give her was too immense to keep giving it without knowing whether or not she was planning on sticking around. And if she had a problem with that, I had to find out sooner rather than later.

In other words, ignorance wasn't bliss any more.

I finished flattening the last row of asphalt, pulled the compactor off to the side, turned off the ignition, and hopped down to the ground.

She was deep in concentration as I approached her.

"Have I told you lately I think you're a genius?" I asked.

She smiled over her shoulder at me. "Not since this morning," she said, her eyes traveling shamelessly up and down my bare chest. "That's a good look for you."

"Thanks," I said, sliding my hands around her waist. "I bet it would be a good look for you, too."

"Get off me sweaty," she said, wriggling from my arms. "I showered this morning."

I smiled. "I remember."

She bumped her shoulder into mine. "You're filthy, you know that? I don't know how I get anything done with you around."

"Likewise," I said, squatting down to close up her paints.

"What are you doing?" she asked, her hands full with her palette and paint brush.

"It's time for a lunch break," I said. "This sun is hotter than you think it is, and you got burned last week."

"But it turned to tan."

"I need to eat," I said, fixing my eyes on her.

"And I need five more minutes."

"Put the paintbrush down, Laney, or there's going to be a Laney sized silhouette across that elephant's face."

She slashed the paintbrush across my chest.

My mouth fell open.

"Okay, okay," she said, squatting slow like a criminal setting down a gun.

"You're going to pay for that," I said, scooping her up and fireman carrying her towards my truck, which was parked in the shady lot beside the park.

"Can I pay you in sex?" she asked.

"With interest," I said, stepping off the sidewalk into the lot.

She let out a little scream and slapped a drumroll on my ass.

I pulled my keys from my pocket, opened the passenger door, and flipped her down onto the seat.

"God it's roasting in here," she said.

I climbed in over her. "If you think it's hot now, you're in for a shock." I pressed my lips against hers and lowered my hips so she could feel how hard I was for her.

She reached over her head, fumbled at the handle on the driver's side door, and pushed it open.

A gentle breeze blew through the front seat.

"Aren't you clever?" I said, kissing down her neck. "Almost as clever as you are beautiful." I reached under her tank top and dragged the front of her bra up over her breasts, kneading them in my hands as I kissed the sweet sweat off them and grew thirsty for the rest of her.

Then I unzipped her little shorts and pulled them down with her underwear.

She dug her hands into my hair as I started circling her clit.

When she let out a sigh, I rewarded her with two thick fingers, glancing up to see the flash in her eyes as I filled her.

"Fuck," she said. "This is already the best lunch break I've ever had."

I smiled and lowered my feet back down to the ground outside the truck so I could lick her warm snatch.

She inhaled sharply as I sucked her sweet silk.

"I want you inside me," she said. "I want to be full of you."

I lapped at her faster and began undoing my jeans.

Then I grabbed her legs, flipped her over, and dragged her ass towards me.

She kicked her feet and stretched her toes towards the ground.

But when I pressed the tip of my dick against her pink slit, she stopped trying to stand and grabbed the front seat, bracing herself as I sank balls deep into her gorgeous heat.

TWENTY SEVEN
- Laney -

He felt so big when he took me from behind, his strong fingers digging into my dangling thighs.

I became wet with sweat as he fucked me, and as my breasts slid against the leather seat of his truck, all I could think about was holding on.

God he was good.

I didn't understand how he could be such a gentleman one minute and such an animal the next. It made me want him so bad it was overwhelming.

I could hear his balls slapping against me as my hair stuck to my face and neck, and he was hitting me so deep I wouldn't have asked him to stop for anything.

Getting fucked by him was the best feeling in the world, and all the minutes in between just felt like unwanted intermissions before he would take me again.

And he never asked. He was polite about everything else, but if he wanted to fuck me it was like nothing could stop him, like this mist of lust descended and made him lose his ability to speak.

It was all in his body language then, especially his eyes. I could see the hunger for me in them moments before he took me. It was like he was already devouring me- like a predator- and there was nothing I could do to stop his mouth watering, nothing I could do to interrupt his hunt.

It made me so high to be wanted like that.

Connor pulled out of me and flipped me over again.

I raised up onto my elbows and scooted back to bring my lifeless legs into the truck.

His hair was a thick mess of blond and several beads of sweat dripped down his rippling chest.

"How do you want me?" I asked, pushing away the wet wisps around my face.

He climbed into the passenger seat and extended a hand.

I pulled myself up and straddled him, wasting no time sliding down his thick cock.

"Who's the sweaty one now?" he asked, unhooking my bra and casting it to the side.

I smiled and rocked against him, my blue eyes lost in his as he groped my breasts and stretched me open.

I dragged a hand down the side of his face and kissed him, causing a bright energy to light me up inside.

He stuck a hand in the sweaty hair at the base of my neck and popped his hips to urge me on, my breasts bouncing against his sticky chest as I focused on the molten heat in my core.

"You feel amazing," he said, his other hand cradling my ass as I rocked against him.

And as I looked into his eyes, I realized we were fucking each other with every part of our bodies, and something happened in my heart. It felt good, like a little crack had opened up and let some light in.

And I realized I still loved him- as much as I ever had- and that I would never stop.

At that point the sweat was nearly dripping in my eyes so I closed them and leaned forward, crushing my chest against his torso as I grinded against the base of his shaft.

"I'm going to come," I whispered against his warm neck. I circled my hips and felt the heat in my body pool in my clit. And when it started to buzz, I knew I was close.

Connor sank his fingers into the fleshy cheeks of my ass. "Melt for me," he whispered, his voice low and liquid.

And I did as he asked, my whole body shaking as I gushed over him like a gutter in a thunderstorm.

"Fuck," I panted, savoring how it felt for my pussy to pulse around his rock hard cock. I don't know where I found the strength then, but I pulled my knees up, planted my feet beside his strong thighs, and began to bounce, my hands anchored around his neck so I wouldn't fall away.

He growled through clenched teeth as I slid up and down him.

I looked down and watched his swollen dick disappear inside me over and over.

When I looked up again, he had a pained expression on his face that told me he was close.

A second later, his hands were on my hips, speeding me up as he furrowed his brow.

Finally, he slammed me down and held me there, groaning as he thrust up into me before letting go, his big hands slapping against the car seat.

I kept rocking against him, milking every last drop as if I were sucking him off. And when my adrenaline crashed, I put my knees back on the seat, buried my face in his neck, and tried to catch my breath.

"I'm so glad I interrupted your work," he said, his head falling against the headrest.

"Me too," I said, leaning back to look at him. "I've decided I like you sweaty."

He smiled. "And I like you wet, but you already knew that."

"Think we could blast the AC for a second?"

He nodded like it was the best idea ever. "Yes, definitely."

I crawled off him and collapsed beside the wheel.

He reached around the passenger side door, pulled the keys out of the lock, and handed them to me.

I put them in the ignition and aimed the vents at us.

"We should probably put our clothes on before we get arrested," he said, grabbing my shirt and shorts off the floor.

"Thanks," I said, sliding the pile near me before leaning forward to grab my twisted bra off the dashboard.

Connor jumped outside just long enough to grab his jeans off the ground and hopped back in, closing the door behind him.

I closed mine, too, and shut my eyes, letting the blast of cool air dry my sweat to my face. "It's too hot to put my clothes on."

"It's too hot to fuck in the car, too, but you managed that alright," he said, wiggling into his jeans.

I rolled my head towards him and smiled. "I did, didn't I?"

"Yes, you're a goddess. Now put on your damn clothes so I'm the only one who gets to know about it."

Since getting caught naked in a public place wasn't a stunt that would help me fit in, I started getting dressed. "What am I going to do about this problem?"

He furrowed his brow. "What problem?"

"The fact that the more I have you the more I want you."

"I'm not the person to ask."

I tilted my head as I connected the tiny hooks on my bra. "Why not?"

"Because all I want to do is enable your addiction."

I smiled. "Seems to me you're in the same pickle then."

"Yeah." He put a bare foot up on the glove box. "I sure am."

"In that case, this is a sticky situation," I said, pulling my shirt on.

"We could always just keep doing what we've been doing and hope we can get it out of our system."

I laughed. "That sounds as fun as it sounds ineffective."

"True."

"And what if we can't get it out of our system?" I asked.

He shrugged. "Then I guess we'll have no choice but to live happily ever after."

TWENTY EIGHT
- Connor -

Her flushed face froze.

"Why are you making that face?" I asked. "Happily ever after isn't part of your master plan?"

"No," she said. "That's not it at all."

"I'm listening."

"I don't have a master plan for one."

"There's a shock."

She turned a palm towards the ceiling. "So what? So I like to go with the wind."

I rolled my eyes. "You like to go against the wind."

"Sometimes it pushes me in the wrong direction."

I rolled my head towards her. "The wind is not to blame for your neurosis, Laney."

"Sorry. I was just startled by how casually you mentioned the happily ever after phrase."

I squinted. "The one that was casually mentioned in every book you read between ages six and twelve?"

She grabbed her hair and held it up with her hands. "Books are different."

"There's only one real difference between books and life."

She raised her eyebrows. "Oh? And what's that?"

"In books the happily ever after is where the story ends."

"Obviously."

"But in real life, you have to keep working on your happily ever after." I dropped my foot from the glove box and turned towards her. "It's a process, a journey. An adventure."

"A Choose Your Own Adventure?"

I shrugged. "If you're doing it right."

"I thought of another difference between books and life."

"What's that?" I asked.

"In life there are never any spoilers. Because no one knows what's going to happen next or how things are going to turn out."

"True," I said. "But doesn't that make life better?"

"Would you want to know the rest of your life?" she asked. "If it were in a book and you could just read the whole thing?"

"Maybe the next page," I said. "But I wouldn't read all the way to the end. What's the fun in that?"

"I suppose it would sort of destroy the adventure part."

"Completely."

She turned the fan down a notch so it stopped blowing the wisps of hair around her face. "What about peace of mind, though? Wouldn't you like to know the future so you could plan for it?"

I shook my head. "No. What if it's not all good news? Then you'd have to waste tons of energy fretting, and I fucking hate fretting."

"No one likes fretting," she said. "It's just one of those things that has to be done."

"I'm not convinced that it is."

"Either way that's not very optimistic."

"I disagree," I said. "If anything, not reading ahead is the most optimistic approach a person could take."

"I suppose I see your point."

"Well cue the marching band," I said. "This is a day I want to remember."

She laughed. "Don't be a smartass."

I reached for a bottle of water on the floor but chose not to drink it when I felt how sickly warm it was.

"So what happens on your next page then?" she asked.

"That's kind of up to you."

"I suppose you did pick last time," she said. "So maybe sandwiches? I've been dying to try the pulled pork from Hanky's-"

"I wasn't really talking about lunch."

"I have to eat, Connor. All I've had today is-"

"You'll get your Hanky's, okay. I just have something else I want to ask you."

She raised her eyebrows. "Sprite?"

"Did you really think the question was going to be about what you want to drink with lunch?"

"No," she said. "You're just making kind of a serious face so I feel a little nervous."

"I'm not making a serious face."

"You are," she said.

"Well you don't have to be nervous, okay?"

"Too late," she said. "Let's get this over with."

I opened the glovebox and pulled out a little velvet box.

She turned an ear towards me.

"I've really enjoyed spending time with you again, Laney-"

"What are you doing?"

"You make me absolutely crazy in a way so fantastic I don't know how I ever lived without you."

She laid a palm across her forehead. "Oh my god."

"And I'm sick of coming up with bullshit excuses just so I can see your face every day."

She swallowed.

I opened the ring box.

I watched her eyes fall to the gold key wedged in the velvet flap. "What is that?"

"It's a key."

"The key to your heart?"

I laughed. "Do you really think I'm that cheesy?"

"I don't know what to think."

I groaned. "It's the key to my house."

She narrowed her eyes at me.

"I want you and Neo to move in with me."

"You what?"

"You heard me."

She craned her neck back. "Don't you think this is all happening a bit fast?"

I shrugged. "No more than I think you could argue that it's happening a bit slow."

"Shit."

"Exciting right?"

She raised her eyebrows. "You're serious?"

"Of course I'm serious. I feel guilty about laughing at Neo every time he runs into that wicker bunny statue."

She laughed. "Me too."

"And I know Helly doesn't like cats in the house."

"No. She doesn't."

"Plus," I said. "I love you."

Her lips fell apart.

"I have since the day I saw you in your geek glasses with your double order of chocolate milk."

She smiled.

"And I think I'm probably a much easier housemate than Helly."

"Easier is one of many words that came to my mind."

I raised my eyebrows. "Along with sexier and more fun?"

"I don't know. Some of Helly's negligees from the seventies are pretty racy-"

"Spare me," I said, raising a hand between us.

"I think that sounds like fun," she said. "And it's incredibly generous of you-"

"I feel a but coming on."

"But I can be a huge pain in the ass."

I laughed.

"What about all my annoying quirks?" she asked.

"Who cares? I have annoying quirks too."

"No you don't," she said. "Tell me one."

I rolled my eyes towards the roof of the truck. "I don't like other people to use my toothbrush."

"That's not a quirk," she said. "That's just normal human nature."

"I don't like cereal," I said. "Except for Frosted Flakes."

"That doesn't exactly make you difficult to live with."

I craned my neck forward. "There are only two decent meals I can make."

"What are they?" she asked.

"Irish stew and spaghetti Bolognese."

"That puts you two major players ahead of me."

"Don't you think it'll be fun?" I asked. "It'll be like when my parents used to go out of town but all the time."

She smiled. "I suppose we have had a few trial runs of living together."

"Don't say yes because you don't have a better offer though." I searched her eyes. "Say yes because it's what you want."

She reached for the little ring box and pulled out the gold key. "I think it is what I want."

I smiled.

"But what if you can't get rid of me once I move in?"

I furrowed my brow. "I hadn't really made a plan for that."

"It could happen," she said, rubbing the key between her fingers. "I'm a lot messier than you."

"That's a quirk of yours I'm already aware of."

"Hey," she said, nudging my shoulder.

"And for the record, I'm not asking you to move in and start doing my laundry and cleaning my house."

She raised her eyebrows.

"I'm a grown man. I don't need any help running my house."

She cocked her head. "So what are you asking me exactly?"

"To share my space because it's brighter when you're in it."

"That's sweet."

"You pushed me."

"And my body," she said. "Don't forget my body."

I laughed. "As if I could. It's only my favorite thing about you."

Her mouth fell open. "What the heck?!"

"So what do you say?" I asked, nodding towards the key. "Is that an adventure you can feel good about choosing?"

She scooted towards me and laid a hand on my cheek. "Of course it is," she said. "And I love you, too."

TWENTY NINE
- Laney -

I couldn't wait to tell Helly the good news.

Hopefully, she wouldn't be too disappointed that I was moving out, especially because I was only going next door.

If anything, I expected her to be relieved. After all, we could still hang out, but she wouldn't feel pressured to think of new ways to tease me about Connor, which I think even she realized was getting pretty old.

Sure, I was nervous about the move, but I was trying not to overthink things.

I mean, Connor didn't have to ask, and I did need a place to live.

Plus, we'd been spending all our free time together anyway, and while I wasn't sure where living together might lead, I had to make progress in some area of my life.

And with each passing day, I was becoming less connected to the idea of a future in New York and more attached to the idea of staying in this quirky little town. I liked waking up to the sound of birds every morning and the fact that people knew my name.

I was starting to feel more centered than I had in a long time.

Plus, Amber's mom let me try my hand at teaching a still life class for her friends, and it went down really well. Sure, it wasn't exactly an exhibit at Moma, but it did give me hope that I might actually be able to make a living from art someday.

And that alone would be a dream come true.

What's more, thanks to Connor's encouragement and the much needed confidence boost I'd gained from doing the mural, I was finally feeling like I had some semblance of control over my life, finally feeling like things didn't have to be so hard, and finally feeling like everything was going to be okay.

Until I saw her.

She was sitting on the couch with Helly drinking tea, and my throat closed up when her eyes met mine.

Her face was like worn leather- hard and soft at the same time- and she looked older than I remembered, older than I ever thought she'd be.

"Laney," she said, rising to her feet.

I couldn't speak. It was like I'd been dropped in a bad dream. My body stayed still but my eyes flitted around the room to the exits, as if I might be able to hack into a different space and wake myself up. Like Beatrice in the Divergent Series.

She walked right up to me and spread her arms.

"Don't," I said, raising a palm and taking a step backwards.

She looked hurt. It wasn't a face I remembered her making.

"What's going on here?" I looked at Helly.

Her crinkled eyes smiled. "Your mom's just out of rehab."

I looked back at the woman with the familiar face. She was wearing a cardigan. A fucking cardigan. And her hair looked like it had been brushed. "That's not my mom."

Her creased lips formed a straight line.

I looked back and forth between her blue eyes. "My mom's a hopeless drunk that wants nothing to do with me."

The woman swallowed. "You have every right to be upset-"

"Don't speak to me," I warned.

She took a step forward.

"Stop," I said, pulling the door open behind me. "You have no right to even look at me."

She nodded. "I know. I'm sorry."

"You don't get to be sorry," I said. "It's too late. Your sorrys don't mean shit."

"Don't speak to your mother like that," Helly said.

I furrowed my brow. "I'm just following the example she set."

"She's been through a lot," Helly said, walking around the coffee table. "She's been through a lot, and she needs our support."

"Fuck that," I said, shaking my head as hatred flowed through me. "And fuck you," I said, staring into the eyes of a mother I'd presumed dead. "And fuck you for letting her in here," I said to Helly before slamming the door.

Then I threw it back open, walked into the kitchen to grab Neo from his bed, and stormed out again, refusing to make any more eye contact with either of them.

I hurried to the end of the driveway, rounded the bushes towards Connor's house, and rang the doorbell over and over until he opened it with an exasperated look on his face.

"What is it? What's wrong?"

"It's my mother," I said, bursting into tears. "She's next door."

Connor put Neo in a carrier box so we wouldn't have to watch him while Sarge got used to his smell. Then he led me to the couch, put a heavy blanket over me, and boiled the kettle without saying anything.

By the time he brought me some tea, I'd finally cried my shock out and could speak between hiccups.

"I take it you didn't tell Helly the good news," he said, pulling my legs across his lap.

I shook my head. "She was just there. On the couch. Drinking tea like everything was hunky dory."

"Did she say anything?"

"I don't remember. I think as soon as she said my name I started screaming." I took a deep breath. "I even swore at Helly for letting her in."

"How did she seem?"

"Tired," I said, wrapping my hands around the steaming mug. "But sober."

He nodded.

"Her eyes were sparklier than I remember, and she looked at me like she could only see one of me."

"Is she staying there?"

"God I hope not. I really can't handle sleeping in the same house as that woman."

"Well you don't have to do that anyway," he said. "Remember?"

"Oh, right."

"And you don't need to ring the doorbell either."

"Sorry," I said. "I just forgot."

"It's fine. I'm sorry I don't know what to say."

"Say I imagined it and that none of this just happened."

"Which part?" he asked.

"The part about my mom showing up and acting like the last time I saw her she didn't throw a bottle at me and call me a stupid slut."

He pursed his lips. "Believe me, I really wish I could."

"Does she think she can just show up and pretend she's been my mom all this time?"

"Maybe she wants to make amends."

"Well, she should've tried that before she tried to hug me."

He raised his eyebrows. "She tried to hug you?"

I rubbed my sore eyes. "I felt cold all over when I realized that's what she was going to do. Numb."

"And how do you feel now?"

"Like puking."

He tilted an ear towards me. "Are you going to puke? Do you need me to get you something in case?"

I shook my head. "No. I'm not. I just wish I could, ya know? It feels like I have all this black hate soaked goop in my guts and it's poisoning me from the inside out."

"Shit," he said. "What can I do to help?"

I sighed. "I wish I knew."

THIRTY

- Connor -

I'd never seen her so distraught.

And I didn't know how to help her.

I couldn't even empathize. I had model parents, the kind of parents that read me bedtime stories and defended me at parent teacher conferences.

Neither of my parents had ever thrown anything at me in my life outside a game of catch. I'd never been locked in my room. I'd never gone to school without a packed lunch. I'd never had to clean up after one of them pissed themselves.

It was hard enough for me to understand how Laney survived that.

So to try and guess how she was feeling now- when she'd carried on like her mom was dead for the last decade- was beyond me.

All I could do was hold her, be strong for her, and keep her safe.

"I can't forgive her," she said, shaking her head against my chest. "If that's what she came here for, I can't give it to her. How could I?"

"You don't have to forgive her."

"What if it's like a step, though? What if she can't move on in her treatment or whatever without my blessing?"

"Tough," I said. "Forgiveness isn't like a parking ticket. You don't earn it just for showing up at the wrong place."

"I almost didn't recognize her," she said, lifting one leg over me so it cut across my thighs.

I reached behind my head and propped a couch pillow up behind me.

"She mustn't still be with that guy," she said. "No one could get sober with him around."

"Mmm."

"Do you think she's still over there?"

I looked at the clock on the mantle over the stone fireplace. "I suppose she could be. She and Helly probably have lots to talk about."

"I hope they're not talking about me," Laney said. "That would really piss me off."

"What if she just leaves town tonight and that's it?"

She craned her neck up and looked at me. "What?"

"What if she's just passing through?"

"Then good luck to her and God bless and good riddance."

"Do you mean that?" I asked.

"Why shouldn't I?"

I shrugged. "You aren't even a little curious about what she might have to say?"

"No," she said, nestling her head back down on my chest. "Do you know what the nicest thing she ever said to me was?"

"What?"

"I was cleaning her up after she puked in her bed, and she looked me in the face and said, 'Maybe having you wasn't a mistake after all.'"

I wrapped my hands around her back and pulled her tight. "I'm so sorry, babe."

"Don't be," she said. "Just don't expect me to forgive her for the bullshit parent she was."

"Okay."

"I was an independent kid," she said. "I'm not saying I wish I were spoiled rotten or anything, but the occasional word of encouragement probably wouldn't have killed me."

"No."

"Do you know what I'm really afraid of?" she asked, lifting her head again.

"What?"

"That she thinks I owe her an apology."

I furrowed my brow. "What the hell for?"

"For abandoning her with that prick and never getting in touch to tell her I was okay."

"You were just a kid," I said. "None of that was your responsibility. Besides, she drove you away. You never wanted to abandon her. You even tried to get her to leave with you."

"I know," she said. "But I could've waited until her wrist healed or something-"

"Her wrist?"

"It was broken," she said. "From a scuffle with Ricky."

"Have I told you lately how amazing I think you are?"

She smiled. "Not in the last few hours."

"Well, for what it's worth, please don't start second guessing the choices you made back then."

"Easier said than done," she said, hugging my chest again.

"Seriously. You did the right thing. You did what you had to do to survive."

"Can't argue with that."

"Besides," I said. "If you hadn't made those choices, I never would've met you."

She poked her head up. "That would be an even bigger tragedy than my childhood."

"Absolutely."

"Thanks, Connor."

"You're welcome."

"You really think it's okay if I don't want to forgive her?"

"I do," I said. "But can I be honest?"

"Please."

"I think you should make an informed decision."

"What do you mean?" she asked.

"I mean if she's around tomorrow, maybe you should consider hearing her out."

"But I don't want to relive everything."

"I'm sure she doesn't either," I said. "But the thing about forgiveness is that sometimes it's actually deserved."

"Uh-huh."

"And other times, it's worth forgiving for selfish reasons."

"Selfish reasons?"

"Yeah," I said. "So you can move on and start to heal or, at the very least, let go of some of that toxic black goop."

She made a pouty face. "I don't know if I have it in me to take such a mature approach."

"It's not about being mature," I said. "It's about doing what's best for you."

She furrowed her brow.

"Think about it," I said. "What's the worst that could happen?"

"She gets sentimental and decides to cuss me out and slap me around to make up for the years she didn't get to."

I shook my head. "No."

"What could be worse than that?"

"Living with regret," I said. "Or living with a bunch of 'what ifs.'"

"You know what I wish?" she asked. "I wish I never asked for your opinion."

"Did I say something wrong?"

She sighed. "No. You said everything right. I just didn't want to hear any of it."

"Sorry."

"Now I can't pretend being mature about it never occurred to me."

"We can if you want," I said.

"No. It's too late. I know it's the adult thing to do."

I pursed my lips.

"She's just the last person I feel like an adult around, ya know?"

"Everyone regresses when they're with family. It's just one of those things."

"I'm going to have to sleep on this," she said.

"Sure."

"But no matter what, I owe my grandma an apology."

I nodded. "At the very least."

"Is Neo still wedged in the TV console?" she asked, squinting across the room.

"He must like it in there because it's warm."

"Where's Sarge?"

"Probably in bed," I said.

"I think that first intro went okay, don't you?"

"I do," I said, scratching her lower back. "I was worried Sarge might play too rough, but I think he can sense that Neo's vulnerable."

She smiled. "Maybe Sarge isn't as dumb as he looks."

"Hey!" I said, tickling her waist.

A moment later, my phone buzzed in my pocket.

Laney sat up so I could pull it out from under me. "Who's texting you at this hour?"

I dragged my thumb across the screen and opened the message. "It's from Helly."

She raised her eyebrows.

"She's just messaging to ask if you're okay," I said, scrolling as I read.

"Uh-huh."

"And to let us know your mom's in room twenty one at the Glastonbury Motel."

FLASHBACK
- Laney -

I heard someone clear their throat and raised my eyes across the table.

Connor was setting out his books, pretending like he didn't know I was right there.

I leaned forward and whispered, "What are you doing here?"

"Trying to study," he said, a sly smile stretching across his face.

"You never come to the library," I said, trying to keep my voice down.

"But you always do," he said. "So I thought I'd come see what the fuss was about."

"Shhhhh!" the librarian glared at us through her cat eye frames.

I pursed my lips.

Connor scribbled something in his notebook and turned it around. "You're hot when you concentrate."

"I am not," I scribbled back.

He grabbed the notebook back and wrote quickly.

When he turned it around again, my eyes scanned the page.

"Meet me in the biography section in two minutes, and I'll prove it."

I lifted my eyes.

He flashed his eyebrows and then got up, pushed his chair in, and disappeared, leaving all his stuff on the table.

I glanced at the clock, the librarian, and the other students hunched over their books with focused looks on their faces.

But when I looked down at my own notebook, it might as well have been an ink spill for how interesting it seemed all of a sudden.

I swallowed and stood up, pushing my chair in quietly. Then I walked up and down a few rows of shelves as if I were looking for something.

Finally, I turned towards the biography section in the back corner.

Connor was standing between the end of a standalone shelf unit and the wall.

"What are you doing?" I asked.

He pressed my back against the end of the thick shelf and kissed me.

I kissed him back, my heart beating through my chest at the challenge of kissing him without making any noise.

A second later, he slid a hand up my skirt and started rubbing my clit through my underwear.

I stopped breathing.

"You're wet," he whispered, his hot breath on my lips as he pulled my underwear to the side.

"That's what happens when someone starts touching me when they're not suppos-"

He laid a palm over my mouth and slid his fingers inside me.

I pressed my head back against the metal shelf, a small moan vibrating up my throat.

"Shhh," he said, his eyes on mine as he fucked me slow.

It felt wrong to feel so turned on at the library, and even though I was freaking out that we might get caught, I found myself arching my back so he could hit me deeper.

My eyes grew wide when I got close.

His focused expression stayed trained on me.

At his house, I had to be quiet when I came so his parents wouldn't hear me, but this was different. The silence in there was so much more intense.

He dared me to come with his eyes, his hand still clamped over my mouth.

I was burning up, and I furrowed my brow as my body clenched around his fingers.

"Now," he said, pressing his forehead to mine and fucking me faster. "Come for me."

I shook and jerked forward, falling against him.

He stayed still and held me up while I tried to catch my breath and waited for the feeling in my legs to return.

When I felt ready to stand on my own again, I wiggled my underwear back into place and smoothed my skirt down. "You're a terrible person," I whispered, scolding him with my eyes.

"Then why are you smiling so hard?" he asked.

I glanced down at his boner and shook my head. "Look what you've done."

He leaned forward and whispered in my ear. "It was worth it, babe," he said. "You can get me back later."

And I did.

And I loved every second of it.

THIRTY ONE
- Laney -

I felt like I was going to choke on my own tongue.

The only reason I stopped myself was because I realized that if I did, my mom might be the one to call the ambulance and she'd end up looking like some kind of local hero.

So I decided it wasn't a good day to forget how to breathe.

But it took me a long time to decide that as I stared at the door to room twenty one.

After the first fifteen minutes, she came out of her room with the ice bucket and went to the machine a few doors down.

I watched her return slowly, her thin hair secured in a low ponytail.

I promised myself that if she was drinking cocktails in there I would walk right back out and not listen to a word she had to say.

Finally, I got out of the car and made my way across the sunny parking lot.

I suppose it would've been more normal to meet her for coffee or something, but I wasn't ready to pretend we were ladies who lunched.

I knocked on the door before I could lose my nerve.

"Laney," she said, as if she were surprised I'd come.

"Hi."

"Come in," she said, stepping back and opening the door.

The room was overwhelmingly beige and worn, like it hadn't been updated in decades.

"Have a seat," she said, gesturing to a desk chair near the TV.

I looked around for booze but didn't see any, nor did I smell it on her. I wondered if she was really sober or if the stench of lemon cleaner was just throwing me off the scent.

She grabbed the ice bucket from the nightstand, popped a flat cube in her mouth, and sat on the edge of the bed.

"What are you addicted to ice chips now?"

She glanced at the tub and set it down beside her. "Sort of."

I sighed. "I suppose that's an improvement."

"You look good," she said.

I hated having her eyes on me, hated her thinking she had anything to do with how good I looked or didn't. "Are you really sober?"

She nodded. "Twenty three months."

"Good for you."

"Thanks." She tucked a wisp of white blonde hair behind her ear, knocking a cigarette onto the bed. "Haven't quite kicked those yet, though."

"Why are you here?"

"I wanted to see you," she said. "And your grandmother."

"I take it Grandma gave you a warmer reception than I did?"

"She tried a bit harder to make me feel welcome," she said. "But she's my mom, isn't she?"

"A mother's love, eh?" I crossed my arms. "I've heard it's supposed to be incredible."

She pursed her lips.

"Why did you want to see me?"

"Well, when your grandma told me how good you were doing-"

I tilted an ear towards her. "Excuse me?"

"We've kept in touch a bit over the years."

I craned my neck back. "No you haven't."

She looked at me in a way that told me there was no use arguing. "Do you really think she never told me you came here? That I didn't know you were safe?"

"You knew I was in Glastonbury from the beginning?"

"Of course I did," she said.

I felt my guts fall through the chair. "You never even sent me a birthday card."

"It didn't seem like a sincere thing to do considering the way things went when I last saw you."

I felt sick.

"Besides," she said. "I didn't think you wanted to hear from me."

"At least you got something right."

"I also promised myself- and your grandma- that I'd be sober the next time you saw me."

I furrowed my brow. "And it took you over ten years to deliver on that promise?"

"It's better than nothing, isn't it?"

I glanced at the floor. "I don't know."

She clasped her hands in her lap.

"So what happened?" I asked. "What made you decide to get your shit together?"

"Ricky got arrested-"

"For what?" I asked.

"Dealing."

"I don't even want to know."

"Anyway, after he went to prison-" Her eyes started to water. "I finally remembered what I looked like without bruises."

I clenched my jaw.

"And I checked myself into rehab."

I swallowed.

"I faltered a few times," she said. "That's why it took me so long to get clean."

"I begged you to come with me."

"I was sick, Laney. And I made a bad choice- one of many."

I scoffed. "No shit."

"But you weren't one of them." She leaned forward. "I know I let you think you were, but that's just because I was so convinced I was going to screw you up-"

"You did screw me up," I said. "And you made me feel like a mistake, like you didn't want me, and like there was nothing I could ever do to be worthy of your love."

293

"I know." She dropped her head and stared at her pale hands. "And I have to live with that."

I rolled my eyes. "You still don't get it. I'm the one that has to live with it. Not you. Me. Every day." I ran a hand through my hair. "Do you have any idea what that's like? And all this time you could've come after me?"

"I know."

"Why didn't you try harder?"

"I was doing the best that I could."

I raised my eyebrows. "That's bullshit. I don't care if you were a young mother. My whole childhood was a disaster. Don't you get that?"

She nodded. "I do."

"Well, I don't know what you were expecting me to say, but I can't pretend I think it's okay for you to show up out of nowhere and act like you didn't fuck everything up."

"I know I fucked everything up," she said, her hands shaking. "And I'm sorry. There are no words that can express how sorry I am. All I can do now is hope you never know the kind of sorrow I feel over the choices I made."

"That makes two of us."

"And if you want to hear that I feel bad, rest assured I do. There hasn't been a day that's gone by since you walked out that I haven't felt bad."

I pursed my lips.

"And not just because of Ricky, who you were right about. Or the booze. Or the things you had to see and do because I was your mother. I know most of it was stuff you never should've been exposed to, much less at that age."

I sat back and let the understatement wash over me.

"But all I can do is apologize and tell you I'm doing my best to get better."

I let my head fall to one side.

"And I'm well aware that it won't be easy, that it will be a long time before you trust me again, a long time before I can say anything nice to you and have you believe it-"

"Good."

"And if you decide the best thing for you is to never see me again, I'll respect that," she said. "Just like you respected my right to not see you-"

"I never respected your right to not see me. I thought you didn't know where I was."

"Fine. Add that to my list of transgressions," she said. "The point is, I just want you to be happy and healthy and loved, and I don't want you to think I ever wished anything but those things for you."

I rubbed my eyes and tried to figure out what to say, tried to guess what I should do-

"Have you finally found happiness with that boy next door?"

I dropped my hands and fixed my eyes on her. "He's not a boy. And you don't get to know about him."

"I already know about him. I've known about him since the beginning."

"Well you don't get to know any more. He's the best thing that's ever happened to me, which makes the two of you oil and water."

"It sounds like he really loves you," she said. "And why wouldn't he? You're a beautiful young woman."

"I forgive you, okay. Isn't that what you want? I forgive you," I said, standing up. "But you don't get to pretend you know me, you don't get to pretend you love me, and you don't get to be part of my life."

She stood up.

"I'm glad you're better, but I didn't need you before you showed up yesterday, and I don't need you now." I opened the door and stepped onto the sidewalk.

She leaned against the doorframe, her face strangely sad and happy at the same time. "Thanks for coming," she said.

And as I walked away, I could feel her eyes on me.

But I didn't look back.

THIRTY TWO

- Connor -

I was worried about her all morning, but it was hectic at the office, and I couldn't even grab a few minutes to check on her.

Plus, I didn't want to smother her. She would come to me when she was ready to talk.

In the meantime, I focused on treating a spaniel who'd ingested rat poison, giving some immunizations to a litter of puppies, cutting the balls off a St. Bernard, and removing a cancerous tumor from a rescue dog.

Needless to say, I was plenty distracted.

But when the phone rang, I lunged for it. "Hello."

"Hey, buddy," Dave said. "You got fifteen minutes to share some burritos? I got an extra with my coupon card and-"

"Sure," I said. "Swing by the office."

As soon as he hung up, I texted Laney. "How did things go?"

She responded a few minutes later. "She's addicted to ice chips and her ex is in prison. Also, she's sorry."

"Well that's something."

"Something is right," she texted.

"You want to talk?"

"Later," she said. "I have to go tear Helly a new one and then apologize."

"Should I even ask?"

"No."

"How about I run you a bath after work?" I typed.

"A bath full of wine?"

"I was thinking rose petals, but wine is easier and cheaper."

"Great," she said. "I'll make dinner."

"Only if you're up for it."

"It's going to be Frosted Flakes," she said. "Don't get excited."

"Too late. Also, you're the best roommate ever."

"Prove it to me with your dick later, and I might think you mean it."

My thumb sped around the screen. "There you go again being such a good roommate."

"Don't forget the wine."

I was relieved to see she was feeling a bit better, or at least, more animated than the numb woman I'd carried from the couch to the bed last night. I just hoped her jokes were proof of progress and not a side effect of her feeling increasingly fucked in the head.

Though my gut told me it was probably both.

After I made sure there were no more animals that needed violated, I met Dave at the picnic table in the field beside my office.

"You're a lifesaver," I said as I sat down across from him. "I was genuinely having one of those days when I was in danger of forgetting to eat entirely."

He raised his eyebrows. "I have no idea what that's like. I plan all my days around food."

"Unless the gangs get on top of you."

"Right," he said, sliding a wrapped burrito towards me. "So what's new?"

"I asked Laney to move in with me."

"No, seriously," he said, unwrapping his lunch.

"Seriously."

His face dropped. "Did you really?"

I nodded and took a bite.

"Why the hell would you do that?" he asked, pulling two cans of soda from the takeout bag.

"Because I love her, man. And I didn't want the woman I love living next door with her voodoo obsessed grandma when she could be relaxing at my place and making it feel like a home."

"Not smart."

"Oh please," I said. "Look me in the eye and tell me you didn't see this coming."

He fixed his eyes on me. "I thought you were smarter than this."

"I don't get why you're so resistant to me letting her back into my life? Is it that you can't bear the thought of sharing me? Are you jealous?"

"That's it," he said, popping his Coke open. "I'm jealous."

"No, really. What's your deal?"

"My deal is that you can't trust her."

"Of course I can."

"How can you be so sure?" he asked. "Love and trust aren't the same thing, ya know."

"But you can't have one without the other."

He cocked his head. "You can apparently."

"I trust her."

"Are you telling me that you're one hundred percent confident that she's not going to break your heart again?"

"I'm not saying that," I said. "But only because relationships don't work like that. Only sociopaths are ever one hundred percent confident about what other people are liable to do."

"Whatever. Are you at least sure she loves you?" he asked. "That you're not just convenient for her? That you aren't hearing what you want to hear and ignoring the rest?"

"Did you come here to piss me off?"

"No," he said. "I came here to bring you a burrito. Because I care."

"Right."

"But you reminded me about something Amber said the other day-"

"Which was?"

"She thinks Laney needs to learn to love herself," he said, taking a big bite.

"What are you talking about?"

He swallowed. "She said you can't love someone else until you love yourself, and she thinks Laney still has some demons."

I clenched my jaw. "First of all, no one loves themselves as much as your wife loves herself."

"Excuse me?"

"So it's ridiculous to hold other people to that standard."

He raised his eyebrows. "My wife is not vain."

I rolled my eyes. "Your wife has been the reigning Miss Vanity for the last ten years."

"That's not even a thing."

"Only because it would be boring for everyone else."

His mouth fell open.

"Second of all, I'm not going to second guess my relationship based on a bunch of shit Amber read on a mommy blog."

"You don't know that's where the idea came from."

I craned my neck forward. "I know it wasn't from a book."

"What are you saying?" he asked.

"I'm saying I don't care if you get it, and I don't need your support."

He tightened his grip on his soda.

"All I want is for you to be happy for me because I'm doing well," I said. "But if you can't find it in your cholesterol clogged heart to do that for your best friend, then I can go without."

"There's nothing wrong with my cholesterol."

"Whatever," I said, shaking my head. "In the beginning, I understood you looking out for me, but now that my relationship has clearly become some weird topic of discussion for you and Amber, I don't really appreciate it anymore."

"Hey," he said. "That's not fair. We've been really welcoming to Laney."

"Have you been, though? Or have you only invited us to stuff because it gives you something to gossip about? Oh look at poor Connor walking into the black widow's web." I pressed my hands against the table. "You don't even fucking know her, okay?"

"I know her enough to know you should've thought twice before inviting her into your home."

I cocked my head. "If you think I didn't think about it more than twice, you're an idiot."

"I didn't come here to piss you off, remember?"

"Well you have," I said, standing up and lifting my legs over the picnic bench. "You're supposed to be happy for me. You're supposed to be supportive. Like I've been of you since you were pissing yourself at sleepovers."

"That only happened twice."

"Once is all it takes to get a reputation."

"Hey- I have been there for you," he said, standing up and resting his knuckles on the table. "I'm the one that was there to pick up the pieces the first time, remember?"

I shook my hands in front of me. "Don't you get it? I don't care if she breaks my heart again. Loving her is the best thing I've ever done."

He sighed.

"If she spent the rest of her life breaking my heart, I'd be the luckiest guy on Earth."

"That's ridiculous."

"And I don't give a shit if she has demons. All I care about is being someone she can count on."

He sat down and put his head in his hands.

"And that's my business," I said. "So you can keep your opinions to yourself from now on."

"Fine," he said, lifting a hand towards me without lifting his face. "I will."

"Good. And for the record, Dave, I'm the one that has to forgive her for what happened before. Not you. Me. And I do. So let it go. It's in the past. And she's my future," I said, walking off. "Whether you like it or not."

THIRTY THREE
- Laney -

The incense hit me like a wall when I opened the door.

"Helly?" I said, coughing.

"I'm in the kitchen," she called.

I made my way through the thick smoke and closed the sitting room door behind me.

"What the heck?" I said. "You can't even breathe in there."

"You wouldn't have been able to breathe in there if I didn't cast out the bad vibes either."

I furrowed my brow. "The bad vibes?"

She turned her back to me and filled the kettle in the sink. "Some woman came in yesterday, cussed everyone out of it, and left an invisible blanket of nastiness over everything, which dulled my crystals and made the cushions suck like leeches."

"I'm sorry."

She glanced at me disapprovingly as she set the kettle on the stove, turning the knob until the clicking sound of the gas stopped.

"I'm not proud of the way I spoke to you."

She shook her head. "And to think I'd been bragging to your mother about what a fine young lady you'd turned into before you arrived."

"I'm sorry I let you down."

"Apology accepted," she said. "But only because I'm not in the mood to treat another room with incense right now."

I sighed and rested my hands on one of the kitchen chairs. "Don't you think you owe me an apology, too?"

She craned her neck back. "For what?"

"For secretly keeping in touch with my mom all this time and not telling me."

She rolled her eyes. "As if you wanted to know."

"That's irrelevant. I had a right to know."

She folded her arms and leaned a hip against the counter. "Your right was to have a safe place to grow up, and that's exactly what you got from me."

"And before?" I pulled the chair out and sat down. "Why didn't you come get me earlier? When you knew how bad things were?"

"I tried," she said. "When you were really little, I tried. But your mom wouldn't accept help, and she was even less interested in hearing reason."

"You could've made her get help."

She cocked her head. "Don't be naïve, Laney. You can't make people do things before they're ready. You of all people should know that."

I tilted an ear towards her. "What's that supposed to mean?"

"It means you know the heartache that comes to people who want their loved ones to be ready for things they aren't."

I swallowed.

She sighed. "Anyway, I tried. But it's hard to stand by and watch your own child destroy themselves through addiction. And when your grandfather fell ill, I couldn't split my energy anymore."

"How long have you been telling her about me?" I asked, crossing my legs.

"Since you first came here."

I narrowed my eyes. "Did she ever write back?"

She hugged herself and dropped her eyes for a moment before lifting them again. "Only when she moved, and then it would only be to inform me of her new address so I would keep telling her how you were doing."

"Seriously?"

She nodded. "She's been writing more since rehab, though."

"About what?"

"Mostly about the things she had to do there and about the memories that came back to her once her mind began to clear. She also apologized for some things that happened before you were born."

"How much does she know?" I asked as the kettle started whistling.

"About you?" she asked, turning off the burner.

I nodded.

"Tea?"

"Please," I said. "Blackcurrant, if you have it."

She made two teas and brought them over to the table, setting them on the stone coasters I'd laid out.

"Well?" I asked, raising my eyebrows.

"I never shared anything you told me in confidence," she said, bobbing her tea bag. "I never shared your feelings or anything. I only told her facts, really."

"Like what?"

"Like how your grades were and what you wore for Halloween and prom. And I might have told her about how mouthy you were the summer I suspected you lost your virginity."

"Grandma!"

She shrugged. "What? Your mother did the same thing. I think a lot of women get bolder once that's happened. I did."

I put my head in my hands.

"It's true," she said. "I figured if I was old enough to invite a penis into my vagina, I didn't have to take any shit from anyone anymore."

I stared at the table. "I'm going to pretend you never said that."

"Fine. And I'll pretend you never drew the same conclusion."

I groaned and leaned back in my chair. "How could you tell her those things when I didn't even know if she was alive?"

"Because you didn't want to know," she said. "You never even mentioned her."

"Still."

"You were becoming a woman, Laney. That's hard enough without having to take on your mom's troubles."

"I can't argue with that."

She groaned. "In that case, I wish I'd mentioned it when you were a teenager. Back then it would've been a treat for you to agree with me on anything."

"I apologize."

"Don't," she said. "That's how I knew I was doing an okay job with you."

I raised my eyebrows.

"I didn't want you to be a yes woman. I wanted you to have spirit, convictions, and an opinion. You didn't always make it easy for me, but I knew you were only being bold because you were growing up and finding your own way."

"You still could've told me recently," I said. "Now that my pathetic excuse for teenage rebellion is out of my system."

She dropped her chin. "Can I be honest with you, honey?"

"Umm yeah." I craned my neck forward. "This whole conversation is about how I wish you'd started being more honest with me ages ago."

She squinted at me. "Based on how little compassion you've shown yourself lately, I wasn't convinced you could handle any more love in your life."

"That woman doesn't love me. And it's not love she wants to give me. It's guilt and shame and disgrace. Like it's always been."

Helly shook her head. "It's love, Laney. And it may be her own brand, but no one can make you feel any of those other things without your permission."

I swallowed.

"Ever since you came here with that Care Bears suitcase, you've only had one real obstacle to happiness, and it's been yourself."

I pursed my lips.

"Not Henry. Not your boss at the diner. Not all those people who didn't give you those covetable jobs in the art world right out of college. It's only ever been you getting in your own way."

"Jesus. Tell me how you really feel."

"Frankly, it's the only concern I have for you and Connor."

"Okay, I was being hypothetical there," I said, pulling my teabag out of the mug and putting it on the saucer. "But now I have to hear the rest of it."

She clasped her hands on the table. "I worry that you aren't happy enough in your own skin yet to accept the love he's capable of giving you, the love he's ready to give you."

"That's not your concern."

"No," she said, pinching her teabag in her fingers and setting it beside her mug. "Just my opinion."

"I don't want you to write my mom any more letters."

"I'll do what I want, Laney."

"Not about me, at least. Please. I'm not comfortable with it."

Helly leaned back in her chair and wrapped her thin fingers around her mug. "I'll agree to that on one condition."

"What is it?"

"That you keep in touch with her yourself."

I shook my head. "How can you ask me to do that?"

"I'm not," she said. "I'm asking you to think about it."

"I don't even know her anymore," I said. "And I didn't like her when I did."

"She's changed."

"So you say."

Helly lifted her mug. "It's obvious when you read her letters."

"Which I haven't."

"I'm happy to give them to you," she said. "If you want."

"You have them?" I asked, a lump forming in my chest.

"Of course I have them. She's your mother."

I bit the side of my lip.

"I figured a day might come when you'd want them."

THIRTY FOUR
- Connor -

I knew Laney was home when I walked in because there was an open box of Wheat Thins in the middle of the butcher block, and the back doors to the porch were wide open.

Outside, she was reclining on one of the sun loungers with a shoe box of letters in her lap.

"What's all this?" I asked, bending to give her a kiss.

"They're from my mom," she said. "To Helly."

I raised my eyebrows and sat next to her crossed legs. "There are a lot of them."

"I guess she had a lot of energy when she stopped drinking."

"How did things go this morning?" I asked. "At the motel?"

"I feel guilty that I wasn't more charitable."

"Don't waste any more guilt on this," I said. "Guilt is such a worthless, unproductive feeling."

"Then why does the church love it so much?"

"Because it distracts people from questioning their faith."

"Shit, Connor."

I shrugged. "You asked."

"True."

"So how did you leave things?" I asked, noticing she was wearing one of my t-shirts.

"I told her I didn't want to see her anymore and that, while I wished her well, I wasn't about to let her back into my life."

I nodded.

"Do you think I'm a horrible person?"

I shook my head. "No. I think it would be horrible if you didn't put your own needs first."

"Really?"

"Of course," I said. "Don't you think the best thing for both of you is for you to do what makes you happy?"

"I never thought about it that way."

I turned away from her and scanned the yard. Sarge was following Neo as he sniffed around the perimeter of the garden, rubbing his cheek on every surface he could find. "How long have they been playing together?"

She shrugged. "About an hour."

"Not bad." I glanced down at the letters. "Just out of curiosity, how is reading her letters not letting her in?"

"Because it's only fair."

I raised my eyebrows. "Fair?"

"Helly's been writing to her about me since I arrived in Glastonbury."

I squinted. "What?"

"She knows about everything. Even you."

"Shit."

"I know," she said. "So it only seems fair that I should know a little about who she is when she's not too intoxicated to express herself."

"You'll take a break if you need to, right?"

She nodded.

My phone buzzed in my pocket.

"Who is it?" she asked.

"It's my folks."

"Tell them I said hi."

I answered the phone and stood up, walking down the steps into the yard to keep a closer eye on Sarge and Neo.

"It's good to hear your voice, Connor."

"You, too, Dad."

"How's the house?"

I glanced over my shoulder at it. "I haven't burnt it down yet."

"Did you call those guys about the double glazing?"

"Not yet."

"What the hell have you been doing?" he asked.

My eyes found Laney and followed her crossed ankles up to where her thighs disappeared into her shorts. "I've been working- and doing that stuff at the park I told you about."

"Oh right. How's that going?"

"Fine," I said. "We're almost done. Then we're going to reinstate Bark in the Park."

"I'm glad there's something in it for Sarge."

"Yep."

"Do you think you could send down a few books we left in the basement?" he asked. "If I told you where they were?"

"How about I send you money instead and you and Mom make a day of buying replacements?"

"I suppose that makes more sense," he said. "I just got so excited she remembered we had them. But you're right, the less time she has to forget she mentioned them in the first place the better. Maybe we'll go tomorrow after golf. Or before golf so I can have a drink at the club..."

I lifted my eyes to the tops of the trees and waited for him to stop rambling.

"Jim McNulty told me you're seeing some girl."

One corner of my mouth curled up. "Jim McNulty's eyes aren't as bad as he makes them out to be."

"Who is she?" he asked. "Someone local?"

"It's Laney."

"Laney Laney?"

I nodded. "The one and only."

"How long has that been going on?" he asked.

"Since before Fourth of July."

"I always liked her."

"I'm glad," I said. "Because she just moved in this week."

"Where?"

"Into the house."

"Holy Cow," he said. "Hold on while I go tell your mother."

I strained my ears to listen.

"Guess what dear? You'll never guess!" he said.

"Just tell me then," my mom said. "I'm too old to play guessing games. My time is too valuable."

"Connor's seeing Laney again."

"Laney Price?" she asked. "Like Next Door Laney?"

My chest swelled at the discovery that my mom remembered her.

"Yep," my dad said. "Isn't that wonderful? She just moved in."

"Where?" she asked.

"Into our house- Connor's house."

"That's great news," she said. "We should send them something nice from Harry & David."

"I don't think they want pears, dear."

"Everyone wants pears! Who doesn't want pears? What's wrong with them?"

"I just think maybe a cake would be better," he said. "Or a pie. We should look and see what else they have-"

"If they know what's good for them, they'll be thrilled with the pears."

"Dad!" I called into the receiver. "Helloo?"

"Sorry," he said, sounding slightly winded. "Your mother is thrilled."

"I heard."

"And she remembers her."

"She is pretty unforgettable," I said, glancing back to see that she'd rolled onto her side and was squinting at the letters with her sunglasses on her head.

"Does Laney like pears?" he asked.

I laughed. "You don't have to send us a housewarming gift, Dad. Save your money."

"I think your mother has her heart set on it."

"Are you sure this isn't one of those times where she insists on getting something for someone because she wants everyone to realize how much she, in fact, wants that same thing?"

"That hadn't occurred to me," he said. "But she does do that."

"At least three times a year."

"Hmm."

"Here's an idea," I said. "How about you tell her you've ordered the pears, but just send them to you instead of us."

"And if she ever thinks to ask, you'll tell her they were juicy and delicious?"

I rolled my eyes. "Of course."

"You're a good man, son. Laney is lucky to have you."

"Thanks."

"I hope she doesn't blow it again."

"Not cool, Dad."

"You know what I mean," he said. "I just hope she's grown up a little. You were both so young."

"I'll keep you posted."

"Please do," he said.

"So don't feel like you have to check back in with Jim McNulty."

"How else will I know what's going on with you?" he asked. "You didn't even tell me you two were dating again."

"Just agree," I said. "And I'll tell him you shot four under par next time I see him."

"Make it six and you've got a deal."

I ran my hand through my hair. "Is there any truth to that or are you still spending all your time in the sand trap?"

"Everyone's allowed a bad game, son. A real man never gloats about another man's off day."

"Really?" I asked. "Because after the game where I shot into the lake twice, you hung a snorkel on the front of the golf cart and told everyone we came across what it was doing there."

"That was hilarious."

"I'm still going to get you back for that," I said. "When you least expect it."

"Bring it, ace. I have a new tee that's totally changed my game."

I laughed. "I'll believe it when I see it."

"Alright, son. Well, thanks for calling."

Had he forgotten that he called me? Oh well. No harm in taking the credit. Might discourage him from having Jim McNulty spy on me. "You're welcome. Love you guys, and call if you need anything."

"Will do," he said. "And tell Laney we said hello. Like I said, we always liked her."

THIRTY FIVE
- Laney -

As much as I'd never admit it, I'd taken Helly's words to heart.

I was my own biggest enemy, and my lack of trust in myself had caused me to choose the wrong man and the wrong work and the wrong path too many times.

But with each passing day, the confidence I had in myself- and my ability to trust my gut- was getting better.

For instance, it was clear that my heart had chosen Connor. Again. And just because I couldn't believe my luck that he loved me back didn't mean I shouldn't be grateful for what we had.

And Neo. Keeping him was down to pure intuition, and that silly klutz had been bringing me more joy and soft cuddles than I ever imagined might fill my days.

The mural was a good thing, too. It had reignited my belief that creativity wasn't just something I wanted, but something I needed. And while I was nervous as hell for Bark in the Park- when the whole town would finally gather to see the finished article- I knew it was a big step forward for me.

After all, I had a professor in school who said art wasn't art until you showed it to someone. Sure, it's something you made and it's wonderful to flex your creative muscles, but he said only by putting yourself out there can you expect the universe to take you seriously and pull you along.

He also thought Picasso came to him in his dreams, but I never claimed to be a good judge of other people's sanity.

So I was doing my best to make progress, no matter what shape it came in.

Unfortunately, not everything was falling into place.

I mean, I didn't want to settle again- like I had with my job at the diner- but I also didn't want to be unemployed.

Following my talk with Helly, I spent two hours floating on my back in the lake trying to pinpoint all the things I was capable of doing that made me feel most loved and most deserving of love.

And being employed was one of those things.

Some of the others included taking the occasional candlelit bath, reading young adult fiction, going for long walks at the nature preserve (Sarge's favorite), and practicing new recipes to surprise Connor with.

But finding a job in Glastonbury was proving harder than I thought, and there was no disputing that it was a more urgent priority than perfecting my fried rice, learning to feign appropriate excitement about Connor's tomatoes, or reading.

Unfortunately, most of the local residents hadn't changed jobs in over a decade, and as one would expect in a small community, the level of nepotism was off the charts.

Still, I'd remained optimistic and had officially dropped my resume off at every single place in town and half of the places in neighboring Sunnyside... except for the funeral homes and the garbage depot.

So far, only two places had called me back.

One was the principal of the local school who informed me that, while they already had an art teacher, she'd be happy to add my name to the end of a dispiritingly long list in case a subbing opportunity popped up.

And the other was someone from Mimi's Café who had just called to get Helly's number since I'd mentioned that I was her granddaughter.

Needless to say, I was feeling a bit deflated by the time I dragged my sore tootsies into the house and kicked my shoes off.

I could hear the shower running upstairs so I headed towards the kitchen to brainstorm what we might have for dinner, greeting Sarge and Neo on my way in.

As I walked around the butcher block towards the fridge, I heard Connor's phone making that horrible dying beep so I grabbed it and walked it over to the charger.

I kept my eye on the screen as I plugged it in to make sure the little battery icon popped up okay, but when the screen lit up, my eyes saw an opened text.

"I'm sorry about that stuff I said about Laney."

I saw Dave's name right before the glowing green battery appeared, and my heart sank.

A moment later, my mind started racing, trying to think of the last time Connor had even mentioned Dave, much less seen him.

I couldn't think of a single time he'd come up since I moved in.

Here I was worrying I might come between random town residents and their favorite librarian when I'd clearly caused friction between the man I loved and his best friend.

I walked up the stairs, feeling a strange mixture of hurt and anger, and opened the bathroom door.

Connor was shaving over the bathroom sink with a towel around his waist.

"Hey babe," he said, dragging the razor up his neck.

"What did Dave say about me?"

"What?" he asked, glancing at me in the mirror.

"I just saw your phone."

He dropped his hand and looked at me.

"It was dying so I plugged it in, and I saw a text from him saying he was sorry about what he said about me."

"It's nothing," he said, turning back towards the mirror. "Don't worry about it."

"What a stupid thing to say."

"Can I finish what I'm doing here?" he asked.

"Sure." I folded my arms. "Be my guest."

I watched him shave for as long as I could before my body started to betray me, and when the desire I felt to run my hands over his muscly chest became too much, I let myself out.

When he came in the bedroom to get dressed a few minutes later- looking freshly shaved and hot as hell- I was sitting on the end of the bed.

"Don't pout," he said. "It's got nothing to do with you."

"It obviously has everything to do with me," I said, crossing my legs so they dangled over the crème colored rug. "You haven't even spoken to him since I moved in."

"Yes I have."

"When?"

He opened a dresser drawer. "The day he pissed me off."

"What did he do?"

Connor pulled his shirt on as he walked over to me and set his hands on my shoulders. "Do we really have to talk about this?"

I nodded.

He sighed. "He thinks I can't trust you."

My shoulders drooped.

"But he's not the one who has to trust you. I am."

I pursed my lips.

"And I do."

"Why?" I asked.

He furrowed his brow. "Why what?"

"Why do you trust me?"

"Because I love you."

I shook my head. "That's not the same."

"It's good enough."

"It shouldn't be," I said, shrugging him off. "Dave's right."

"Don't be ridiculous."

I squinted at him. "Why are you so willing to give me another chance?"

He folded his arms but stayed standing in front of me. "I just told you."

"But you've never even asked why I said no. You've never even asked me not to do it agai-"

"I don't want to push you, Laney."

"Well maybe you should!"

He shook his head. "Pushing you is what made us lose out on so many years together."

"No it's not." I pulled my legs up to sit cross legged. "I'm the reason we lost out. It has nothing to do with anything you did."

He clenched his jaw.

"Dave's right."

Connor's lips twitched. "He's not."

"Yes he is," I said. "He's right about the fact that I don't deserve your forgiveness, and he's right about the fact that you need to demand more from me."

"Tough," he said. "Because I forgive you. And I think you demand enough of yourself without me piling on."

"I don't," I said. "I never have. I'm a total coward."

His lips fell apart.

"And I'm doing my best to be the kind of woman I want to be, the kind of woman who's deserving of a man like you," I said. "But I need you to hold me accountable. I don't want to break any more promises. Not to myself. And especially not to you."

"Okay," he said, pulling me into a hug. "Okay."

"Promise you'll be harder on me," I said, pressing my cheek against his chest. "And don't let me off the hook so easy."

"Shhhh," he said, smoothing my hair down.

"And make me earn your trust again," I said. "For both our sakes."

THIRTY SIX
- Connor -

I unlocked the door and pushed it open so Laney could go inside first.

Sarge came rollicking up to her a second later. I swear I kept thinking I had him housetrained when she wasn't around, but every time he saw Laney, he tried to climb her.

It was as frustrating as it was endearing.

"Can I get you a glass of something?" I asked, locking the door and noticing Neo stretched out halfway up the stairs.

She turned around and slung her arms over me. "That was the best birthday dinner of my life," she said, kissing me. "I can't believe you took me somewhere so fancy."

"It was the only place I could find around here that could make you a dirty martini."

"I suppose I have been going on about craving them for a few weeks."

"I'll learn to make them," I said, hoisting her up.

She wrapped her legs around my waist.

"Then you can have them to your heart's content."

She hugged me as I walked to the kitchen. "That would be a lot of martinis."

I set her down on the butcher block. "You have one more birthday surprise."

She flashed her eyebrows. "I hope it's your dick."

"I misspoke there," I said, taking off my sports jacket and laying it on the counter. "You have two more birthday surprises."

She cocked her head and twirled a finger around the buttons of my shirt. "Besides the one that's not a surprise anymore?"

I nodded. "Correct."

"I told you I didn't want anything."

"Well, you talk so much I have to tune some stuff out so I guess I didn't hear you."

She pushed my chest and wobbled slightly on the counter. "Lucky me."

"Are you ready?" I asked.

"I'm never ready for anything when it comes to you," she said, kicking off her shoes. "But you haven't let me down yet."

"Come on," I said, taking her hand and helping her down from the counter.

Her dress slid up her thighs as she hopped to the ground, and she smoothed it over her hips before following me.

"Right this way," I said, heading down the hall.

"Is it a pony?"

"I hate to disappoint you, but after seeing how much you struggled with cleaning Neo's ears, I'm not sure you're ready for a pony."

"Party pooper," she mumbled. "Is it a pink convertible?"

I looked over my shoulder. "Since when do you want a convertible?"

"Since I got a hot boyfriend that I like to show off."

I smiled. "I'll look into it."

"Is it a swimming pool?"

"What do you need a swimming pool for when we live so close to the lake?"

"First of all, they're totally different things," she said. "And second of all, I already told you I don't need anything so how should I know what to guess?"

I stopped outside the door to my dad's study.

She twisted her face. "Is it one of those globes you put pins in when you visit places?"

I raised my eyebrows. "Are you done?"

She nodded.

"Close your eyes."

She groaned.

"And no peeking."

She squinted at me.

"I can still see your eyes, Laney."

"Fine," she said, squeezing them shut.

"How many fingers?" I asked, holding some up.

"I don't know. My eyes are closed."

"Just checking," I said, pushing the door open. Then I took her hand. "Keep them closed until I say."

"I'm freaking out, Connor."

"Freak out with your eyes closed," I said, coaxing her a few more steps.

"Can I open them yet?"

I laid a hand on her lower back. "I'll give you a countdown."

She pursed her lips.

"Ninety nine, ninety eight-"

"Don't be a smartass."

"Three, two, one."

Her eyes popped open and her lips fell apart.

I watched as her eyes bounced around the room.

It was filled with canvases and paints and her easel from Helly's shed. There was a special mat on the floor so she could make a mess if she wanted, and I'd pushed my dad's desk against the wall and converted it into a place where she could store all her brushes and supplies.

"Oh my god," she whispered, raising her fingers to her lips.

"What do you think?"

"Is this-?"

I stepped up beside her. "It's your very own studio."

"What if you need to do some work?"

"I'm fine at the kitchen table," I said. "Besides, this room has the best light."

She shook her head. "I'm in shock."

"Good shock?"

She nodded, walked up to the easel, and ran her palm along the wood. "This is my old easel."

"It is," I said. "But all the paints and brushes are new and-"

"I can't believe you went to all this trouble."

"It was a pleasure."

"Aren't you worried I'll never find a job if I have a bitchin' studio to hang out in?"

I shook my head. "No, and I know how hard you've been trying to find a job-"

She looked over her shoulder at me. "You do?"

"Of course I do. It's a small town."

She dragged a bare foot across the mat beneath her. "I do have to find something though."

"You will," I said. "But you shouldn't just take anything."

"I would-"

"I know," I said, hooking my thumbs in my pockets. "I figured that out when Timo called for a character reference."

Her face dropped. "What did you say?"

"I told him not to hire you."

Her eyes grew wide. "You didn't."

"I did," I said. "I'd rather you were painting than bartending, and I know that's what you'd rather be doing, too."

"You can't do that."

"I already did," I said. "But I've also thought a lot about what you said about me going too easy on you, and I think you're right."

She tilted her head at me.

"Which is why I made a deal with the manager at Mimi's Café and Mason's flower shop that you'd have three paintings done for each of them before the end of September."

She craned her neck forward. "What?"

"If they sell, they sell, and if they don't, someone's bound to see them in one of those places and commission something."

"What if I say no?"

"Let's not play that game," I said. "I know you're up for the challenge."

She pursued her lips and nodded. "You know, I think I am."

I smiled. "How's that for pressure?"

"So you're really serious?"

"Of course, I'm serious," I said, stepping up to her and sliding my hands around her waist. "The happiest I've ever seen you was that summer you painted until you had blisters."

"That's not true," she said, hooking her hands around my neck and leaning against me.

"Sure it is."

She shook her head. "No. I'm happier now."

I dropped my forehead against hers. "Me too."

"Thanks," she whispered, her warm breath on my lips.

"You're welcome, babe. Happy Birthday."

"You know what would make my birthday even better?" she asked, unbuttoning my shirt buttons.

"What?"

"If you were in a better mood."

"What?" I craned my neck back. "I'm in a fine mood."

She shook her head and dropped her hands to my belt. "I'm not convinced. You seem tense."

I went stiff all over as she lowered my zipper. "Now that you mention it, I have been under a lot of pressure lately."

She pushed my pants down.

"And by lately, I mean ever since I saw you put on the panties you're wearing under that dress."

"That's what I thought," she said, giving me a kiss. "Besides, my new studio needs christening."

THIRTY SEVEN
- Laney -

I kept my eyes on his as I started stroking him, tearing them away just long enough to find a chair.

I smiled to myself when I saw the one behind him. It was the cozy one from my room in Helly's house that I'd found at a yard sale when we were fifteen.

I fell in love with how dated it was and how cocooned I used to feel when I sat in it, as if the curved shape of the tall back could keep my thoughts from spilling out over the sides.

It was the chair I would've put in here if he'd asked me, and I loved that he knew me so well.

But it didn't look very big when he sat his bare ass down on it, his broad shoulders as wide as the back of the chair.

"Fuck, Laney," he said, grimacing as I stroked him and dropped to my knees. "I didn't know you needed a muse, too."

I smiled and flicked the tip of his head with my tongue. "I am going to make you come so hard," I said, pulling my little blue dress off over my head and keeping my eyes on him as I undid my bra. "And you can paint me wherever you want," I said, stroking him again. "The back of my throat. My chest. My ass."

He leaned back in the chair and gripped the armrests until his knuckles went white.

Then I sank my mouth down on him.

After only a few bobs, my jaw felt sore from being opened so wide- just like it used to when I'd suck him off under his Major League bedspread.

I moaned and he swore, sliding his hips forward as he swelled in my mouth.

When I needed a break, I kept stroking him and licked his balls, sucking them into my mouth like grapes and moaning until he pushed his head back against the chair.

Then I took him deep in my throat again, sliding up and down his solid shaft as the blood pumping through him coursed against the thin skin of my wet lips.

A moment later, he grabbed a fistful of my hair, pulling it so tight my scalp tingled. "Faster," he said, spreading his hand over the back of my head.

I was sucking him so hard it scared me, but I couldn't stop. I wanted his release inside me so bad, and it turned me on that his hand was keeping me from coming up for air.

"Yeah," he said, growling as his hips rocked.

I tried to go faster, tried to go so fast he'd feel like he was fucking my mouth.

And in the end, he did- with one final thrust that stuffed my throat right before I felt his orgasm burst through him and into me.

I drank him greedily then, milking him down my throat as if I craved his seed more than my next breath.

When I'd swallowed every last drop, I looked up and wiped the corner of my mouth on the back of my hand.

He reached forward and grabbed my arm. "Get up."

I rose to my feet, but I was so turned on from sucking him I couldn't see straight.

"Turn around."

I did as he said and felt his hands on my hips a moment later, pulling my panties down until they fell to the floor. Then he pulled me back and probed my slit with his dick.

I slid down on it as soon as it touched me.

He reached forward and lifted my legs over the arms of the chair. Then he moved one hand to my clit and the other to my breasts, slouching down so I had no choice but to lie back on him and let him have his way with me.

My limbs were lifeless as he fucked my core, and as he rubbed my clit into a buzzing frenzy, I dug my head back against his shoulder and felt my body clench around him.

"God that feels good," I said as he brought me to the brink.

My clit was throbbing under the pressure of his fingers, and he groped my breasts with such force that my nipples became so hard they ached.

"Come for me, Laney," he said, massaging my g-spot with his dick.

I closed my eyes and felt the heat in my body pool where he was stretching me open and circling my clit. "I'm going to come," I whispered into his neck.

I arched my back and shook a moment later, my orgasm crashing through me like a flood.

He slowed the movement of his hips, riding out the pulsing waves that radiated from my center as he loosened his grip on my breasts.

"That was amazing."

"Yeah," he said. "Even better than the fantasy I had about having you on the table at the restaurant."

I turned my head to look at him. "Is that what you were thinking about when you stopped listening to my rant about global warming?"

"You ranted about global warming?"

I pretended to elbow him in the ribs. "Very funny."

"It was actually a pretty intense fantasy. I was going to secure your hands by forking your bracelets to the table. Then I was going to titty fuck you before the dessert course-"

"Jesus."

"And come on your chest- maybe even your dessert, if you were up for it."

I laughed. "How about outside this house, I'm the painter in the family?"

"I can't control my thoughts, Laney."

I stood up and turned around so I could straddle him and see his face. "It doesn't sound like you were trying very hard."

"You started it."

I furrowed my brow. "How?"

"When I saw you spray perfume between your tits when we were getting ready to go out."

"You weren't supposed to see that."

He raised his eyebrows. "Did I mention your tits were out?"

"Still."

"Well, I refuse to unsee it. It was the most interesting thing I've seen all week."

"Consider it a gift then."

"Oh I do."

I rolled my eyes.

He pushed some hair out of my face. "I can't wait to see what beautiful things you make in this room."

"I'm really excited," I said, looking over my shoulder at my officially christened studio.

"I picked up on that," he said. "Despite the subtle way you said it."

One side of my mouth curled into a smile.

"So birthday girl, what do you want to do with the rest of your big day?"

"Hmm." I cocked my head. "Is drinking until we have the energy to do that again an option?"

"I suppose it will have to do since I'm all out of surprises."

"I don't believe it." I trailed my fingertips down his chest. "You? Out of surprises?"

"Crazier things have happened."

"True," I said. "But all the craziest things happen when I'm with you... so I have to believe the best is yet to come."

"You think things could actually get better than this?" he asked.

"I don't know," I said, smiling. "All I know is that, for the first time in my life, I can't wait to stick around and find out."

THIRTY EIGHT
- Connor -

Bark in the Park was a massive success. I figured it would be because slushies and dogs and dunk tanks usually make for a good party, but the turnout was far grander than I thought.

People came from all the surrounding towns, and the raffle prizes got so big some of the winners cried- including the kid who won the Around the World Basketball Shoot Out and announced that he was going to spend his winnings on an Xbox with such emotion one might have thought an Xbox was a long awaited refugee food parcel.

Meanwhile, the winner of one year's worth of discounted vet care went to Jim McNulty and his three Lurchers, which meant I could count on my folks hearing all about the success of the day.

Best of all, loads of people kept coming up to Laney, telling her what a nice job she did with the mural, and thanking her for her hard work.

So to say I was beaming as we stood in the fenced off green space watching Sarge sniff a poodle he'd never met would be a huge understatement.

"Would it be weird to admit I'm kind of emotional?" Laney asked, sucking some red slushee from her crazy straw.

I shook my head. "Not at all," I said, going for my straw before I remembered my brain freeze hadn't completely worn off from my initial enthusiasm. "It's been a much greater success than I think anyone could've anticipated."

"I thought you'd be better off without me."

I tilted an ear towards her. "What?"

"That day in the park all those years ago."

I swallowed.

"I thought you'd be better off without me."

I furrowed my brow. "Why are you telling me this now?"

"Because I should've explained myself a long time ago," she said. "I just didn't know how to."

"You don't have to say anything."

"Yes I do," she said, standing still while a strange bulldog sniffed her painted toes.

"Well, I don't know why you thought that."

"Because," she said. "I was young and scared shitless and I felt unworthy of your love."

"But it was so sudden. You never felt unworthy before."

"Yes I did."

I clenched my jaw.

"I just didn't have the strength to admit it to you. Or me."

"Why would you think I'd be better off without you? We were so good together."

"I thought I'd hold you back," she said, her eyes following Sarge. "I thought you were destined for bigger and better things and that you'd go to California and feel like you made a horrible mistake."

I searched her blue eyes.

"And I'd turn into some kind of security blanket you were embarrassed about and didn't want to sleep with any more and-"

"As if I'd ever not want to sleep with you."

She craned her neck forward. "You know what I mean."

"I don't," I said. "But I appreciate you being honest with me."

"Good. Because it kind of hurts to admit that I was scared shitless and insecure."

"I forgive you."

"Genuinely?" she asked. "Like you don't even have one tiny little shred of resentment?"

"No." I took a sip of my blue slushee. "Don't get me wrong, I was heartbroken. But I was also grateful for every day we had together, and I wasn't about to poison those memories by holding a grudge."

"You're a better person than I am."

"Not better. Just more mature."

Her mouth dropped open. "Excuse me?!"

"I'm joking," I said, a sly smile escaping as I glanced at her out of the corner of my eye.

"It would be immature of me to argue with you about that so I'm not going to," she said. "But that's the only reason."

I laughed. "As long as you have your reasons."

She shook her hair back behind her shoulders.

I took a deep breath. "Can I ask you just one question?"

She nodded.

"Do you feel differently now?"

Her eyes smiled. "I do."

"So you're over all that bull?"

She tilted her head. "You mean do I still feel unworthy and scared shitless and like I'm holding you back?"

I nodded.

"No," she said.

"I'm glad," I said. "Because I'd really hate to have to drop my slushee and sing 'Wind Beneath my Wings' in front of all these people just to convince you of your worthiness."

"I don't know who would die of embarrassment first if you did that."

I raised my eyebrows. "What if I went with 'When a Man Loves a Woman'?"

"I would still drop dead right here in the dog park."

"Can this be one of those times when it's the thought that counts?"

"Yes," she said, putting her hand on my shoulder. "It can definitely be one of those times."

"Cool. As long as I get the points."

"You can have all the points," she said. "Just don't sing to me in front of everyone with those blue lips."

I licked them. "Oh shit are they that blue?"

"Like a baboon's butt."

I pursed my lips and rubbed my tongue across them as hard as I could.

"Don't worry about it," she said. "I probably look like I'm bleeding from the mouth."

"You don't," I said. "You're lips look puffy and pink and kissable as ever."

She smiled. "I have been careful."

"Damnit."

"Howdy, folks," Dave said, appearing on the other side of Laney.

"Hi," I said.

"I just wanted to congratulate you two on making this awesome party happen. The kids have had the best day, and I even won a free hot shave," he said, raising a coupon in the air.

"No problem," I said, wishing Laney had never seen that text and that the air between us hadn't gone so tense.

"Dave," Laney said, turning towards him. "I think we need to clear the air. Maybe start over?"

"Excuse me?" he asked, looking nervously back and forth between us.

"It's come to my attention that you have some concerns about whether or not Connor can trust me," she said.

Dave shot me a look.

"And I think you have every right to feel that way," Laney continued.

He furrowed his brow. "You do?"

"Of course," she said. "I know you have his best interests at heart and that you'd never deliberately try to make trouble for him."

He shook his head. "No. Of course not."

"And I just want to assure you that I'm doing everything I can to earn his trust again."

I swallowed.

"But." She set a hand on his shoulder. "I also want to know what it would take to earn your trust again because the last thing I want is to come between you guys when you were friends a long time before I showed up."

I couldn't believe she was calling him out like this. The poor guy was never good with confrontation. If I didn't know him so well, I would've been laughing at how visibly uncomfortable he was.

"Don't put your tail between your legs in the dog park, Dave," I said, beaming with pride at my little firecracker. "Answer the woman."

THIRTY NINE
- Laney -

It felt great to know Connor had my back, but the last thing I wanted was for Dave to be uncomfortable.

Scratch that- the last thing I wanted was for him to ever talk shit again- but his being uncomfortable came right after that.

"I'm sorry, Laney," he said. "It was never within my rights to second guess him."

"Sure it was," I said. "That's what any good friend would've done."

"But I could've been more supportive," he said, moving the balloon animal he was holding behind his back. "I see that now."

"Seriously, Dave. What can I do to earn your trust again?" I asked. "What can I do to make you believe that I'm happy here and that Connor doesn't need to worry about me doing a runner again?"

Connor flinched.

"Nothing," he said. "I was out of line. I said those things in confidence." He shot Connor another look. "Not to make you uncomfortable."

"That's not an answer," I said, eager to make a deal, shake on it, and call this little misunderstanding- albeit deserved- water under the bridge.

He shook his head. "My wife and kids are already crazy about you, Laney. That's more than enough for me."

"Well it's not enough for me, and it's you I need to impress," I said. "So pick something. Anything."

He looked at Connor and received an encouraging nod before biting the inside of his cheek. "I guess I could use some help painting the treehouse I just put in."

"Perfect."

Connor raised his eyebrows. "You caved?"

"Sometimes it's easier to just give in to women," Dave said, patting him on the arm. "Trust me."

"When do you want to do this olive branch treehouse painting?" I asked, sipping my slushee.

"How about next weekend?" he asked.

"Perfect," I said. "I'll look forward to it."

Connor pulled his phone out and slid his thumb over the screen.

"Thanks, Laney," Dave said. "And I apologize again for overstepping-"

"Don't worry about it. It's in the past," I said, extending my hand. "I'll forgive yours if you can forgive mine."

He took my hand and pulled me into a hug, patting my back with the balloon animal. "Deal."

When we stepped back again, Connor was staring wide eyed at his phone.

"What is it?" I asked, resting my free hand on his shoulder. "Is everything okay?"

"It's my patent."

Dave and I craned our necks forward.

"It's been granted."

"Holy shit!" I said, jumping in the air and then covering my mouth when I saw the faces of the horrified mothers around me. "Are you serious?!"

"I'm as serious as handicapped dogs walking again," he said, handing me the phone.

Sure enough, there was an email from his lawyer that was filled with lawyer speak but clearly contained the words "your patent has been approved and granted."

"What does this mean?" I asked.

He shook his head, still obviously stunned. "It means thousands of injured animals all over the country are finally going to get the treatment they deserve."

I laughed. "I understand the bottle stopper thingy, but what does it mean for you?"

"Money," Dave said. "Lots and lots of money."

Connor ran his free hand through his thick blond hair and exhaled.

"Looks like we'll be serving champagne at the treehouse painting party," Dave said.

Connor raised a palm. "You don't have to do that."

"Of course I do," he said. "This is the best thing you've done since you put a crab in Miss Martine's desk."

The corner of my mouth curled up. "I can't believe you used to be such a bad boy."

"I can still be a very bad boy," Connor said, flashing his eyebrows and sliding a hand around my waist.

"That's my cue to leave," Dave said. "I'll see you guys next Saturday."

We smiled and nodded, turning towards each other as he walked off.

"I'm so proud of you," I said, laying a hand on Connor's cheek.

"I'm kinda proud of me, too," he said.

"You should be."

"It's a weird feeling, though," he said.

I furrowed my brow. "What is?"

"Wanting something so bad for so long and then getting it all of a sudden."

"I know."

"Yeah?" he asked.

I nodded and fixed my eyes on his. "I have to deal with that feeling every day."

He smiled. "I didn't think this day could get any better."

"I did."

"You did?"

"Of course," I said. "Anything can happen when I'm with you."

He kissed me, and I felt one foot rise out of the grass.

"Excuse me," a frail voice said.

I opened my eyes and unhooked my lips from Connor's. "Can we help you?" I asked, turning towards the little old lady. She was wearing a purple sundress and a pair of glitter covered Keds.

"I'm sorry to interrupt," she said. "But it was either that or join in."

I suppressed a smile.

"Are you the woman that painted the mural?" she asked.

"I am."

"Well-" She extended a card in my direction. "I'm an artist, too."

"I see that," I said, admiring the card which had Gwendolyn Brooks written on one side and the image of a Monet-esque oil painting on the back.

"I don't know if you've heard of me-"

I glanced at Connor.

"But I'm the artist in this town."

"Okay," I said, raising my eyebrows.

She shook her head. "And this town isn't big enough for two artists."

I tilted an ear towards her.

"Fortunately for you, dear, I'm riddled with arthritis." She raised her hands as if I might be able to see it everywhere.

"I'm sorry to hear that."

"Don't be." She waved her hands at me and dropped them again. "They had a good run."

I sipped my slushee until a big slurp echoed through the striped cup.

"Anyway," she continued. "I was hoping you could help me out."

I pursed my lips. "I'm not sure I understand."

"I'm the one that paints the windows in this town," she said. "Every season I use special paints, and I decorate the bank and the post office and the elementary school and the record shop and the bakery and, well, you get the idea."

"I do."

"And then I scrape all the paint off and do it again when the next season rolls around."

I raised my eyebrows. "Wow."

"I do special holiday gigs, too."

I prayed that she would get to the point.

"To make a long story short, I can't keep up with it anymore."

I tucked some hair behind my ear. "It does sound like a lot of work."

"Basically, I was wondering if I could give my clients your number," she said. "Because even though it saddens me that I can't go on, it would kill me more to think no one would bother to keep painting the windows."

I craned my neck back. "You want me to do it?"

She nodded. "The businesses will pay you, of course."

"Right."

"Except for Juno at the bakery," she said. "But you'll never need to buy bread again."

"Why me?"

She shrugged. "Because I asked around, and everyone said if anyone could do it, you could."

I felt a lump in my throat. "Really?"

"No," she said. "This is my idea of a hilarious joke. I'm actually a professional tap dancer."

"Right," I said. "Got it."

"What do you say?" she asked.

"Thank you so much," I said, throwing my arms around the woman before gently hugging her delicate frame.

"You're welcome dear." She patted me on the back.

I gave her space again.

She raised a finger at me. "Your good hugs won't be enough, though," she said. "You're going to have to paint your ass off."

My eyes grew wide.

"The people of Glastonbury have very high expectations because of the standards I've set."

"I won't let you down," I said, slipping the card in my pocket.

She nodded at Connor and then me again. "I look forward to hearing from you."

"Whoa," he said after she walked away.

"Whoa is right."

"I thought she was going to draw a pistol for a second there when she was all 'this town isn't big enough for the both of us.'"

"Me too."

"Well that's lucky."

I searched his eyes. "Did you know that was going to happen?" I asked. "Have you been going around behind my back and asking people to say nice things about me?"

"No." He shook his head. "That was all you."

FORTY
- Connor -

Laney had dragged one of the sun loungers off the patio into the yard and had been sketching away wildly for hours.

It was approaching dusk and bright colors were starting to rise in the sky over the tall trees in front of her, and Sarge was still lying under her chair, his paws moving occasionally when he fell into a puppy dream.

Meanwhile, Neo was sprawled out next to Laney's feet, his little grey head resting on his arm as he basked in the fragrant summer air.

I watched the scene from the window as I opened a chilled bottle of Laney's favorite white wine and wondered what I did to get so lucky.

A year ago I moved into this big house all by myself, and at the time, it felt empty apart from my childhood memories.

Sarge took the edge off, of course, bringing noise and laughter back into the house, but never in my wildest dreams could I have imagined how full of love my home might be so soon after.

Okay, maybe in my wildest dreams, but I didn't pay them much mind.

I was a realist at heart, and I knew it was unlikely that I'd get a second chance with the woman who taught me what it meant to love someone.

But like Laney always insisted, life truly was full of surprises.

I poured two glasses of wine and walked barefoot through the grass to the middle of the yard where she was sitting, just out of reach from the shade of the apple tree my dad and I planted when I was only as tall as the shovel itself.

Before interrupting, I took a moment to admire her concentrating face, her delicate features all scrunched and aimed at the paper, and her small hands, which struggled to hold six different colored pencils at once because they didn't fit behind her ears with the rest of them.

"Lovely evening," she said without looking up.

"So you're not out here missing the big city?"

I saw her cheeks rise with her smile. "No," she said. "But if I ever do, just turn on that killer sprinkler of yours and let me run through it a few times in the grass. That should sort me right out."

"Deal," I said, extending a glass into her field of vision.

"Ohh!" she squealed. "What a nice surprise!"

"You're welcome," I said, lifting Neo with one hand so I could take his spot at the end of the chair before draping him over my lap.

"Cheers," she said, clinking her glass against mine.

"What will we toast to?" I asked, my eyes on her light blue ones.

She twisted her mouth and rolled her eyes up in thought. "To long summer days?"

I nodded. "I'll drink to that."

Neo rolled onto his belly and started sniffing the air so I set him in the grass.

"Did he just collapse next to Sarge?" Laney asked a second later.

I bent over and looked under our chair. "Right against his belly."

She smiled. "They crack me up."

"What are you working on?" I asked.

She looked down at the notebook and scratched her head. "I'm trying to figure out what to put in the windows at the school."

"Oh yeah?"

"Gwendolyn told me she usually does pencils and staplers and school supplies, but that doesn't seem very exciting to me."

"Yeah, well, the first day of school isn't very exciting for most people."

"I know," she said. "That's why I want to put some thought into it."

"I'm sure you'll come up with something."

She nodded and dropped her pencils in the grass, followed by the oversized notebook. "I appreciate the vote of confidence."

"No problem."

"I can always count on you for that."

"You done for the night?"

"Yeah," she said, smiling at me. "I'd be a fool to keep working with a view like this."

I laughed and looked down at the grass around my feet. "I think I can do you one better."

"I don't know," she said. "This is a pretty dynamite setting."

I set my glass beside the chair, turned towards her, and dropped to one knee. "Laney," I said, fixing my eyes on her. "There's something I've been wanting to ask you."

She straightened up a bit.

I reached in my back pocket and pulled out the familiar ring. "Having you in my life again has been a dream come true, and I can't imagine spending the rest of my days with anyone else."

Her eyes went wide.

"There is nothing I want more than to care for you, encourage you, and drive you crazy in all the ways I know how and all the ways I haven't yet discovered."

She pursed her lips.

"Since the beginning, we've been choosing our own adventures, and I have no idea what life has in store for us. All I know is that I want my every next page to have you in it."

Her eyes started to water.

"I love you with everything I have for everything you are, and I would wait for you forever. But I'd rather die tomorrow knowing you were mine than live one more day hoping you know how much you mean to me."

She turned towards me and tucked her feet behind her.

"I love you, Laney. Marry me already."

Her face sprang into a wide smile. "I thought you'd never ask."

I slipped the ring on her finger and held her hand as she bent down to kiss me.

When we came up for air, she rested her forehead on mine and her voice fell to a whisper. "I can't believe you still have the ring."

"I can't believe that surprises you."

She patted the chair and I took a seat beside her.

"I'm sorry I didn't say yes the first time," she said, leaning against my shoulder.

"Don't be," I said. "What matters is that you said yes this time."

She raised her eyebrows. "And if I hadn't?"

"Are you trying to ruin the moment?"

"Sorry."

I smiled. "It's okay."

"I actually think we should drag out the moment as long as possible."

"How do you propose we do that?" I asked.

"Well," she said, admiring the ring on her finger. "You know all that stuff you said about the pages?"

"By heart, obviously."

She laughed. "I have a question."

"Shoot."

"I have every confidence that I'll always want to read the next page knowing you're in it."

"That would be even sweeter if I hadn't just said that."

She blushed. "I know, but is it possible to reread bits we really liked?"

"What do you mean?"

"Like, what if I wanted to reread that part from last weekend?"

I furrowed my brow. "You're going to have to be more specific."

"When you joined me in the shower?"

My eyes grew wide. "You liked that, did you?"

She nodded. "Very much."

"I think that can be arranged."

"I thought you might say that," she said, taking a sip from her glass.

I sighed. "You'll have to give me a minute, though. I'm a bit high right now over the fact that you're going to be my wife."

She laughed and her eyes sparkled. "Take all the time you need," she said. "I'm not going anywhere."

Epilogue
Laney

Dear Mom,

I'm glad to hear you found a nice roommate and that she's sober, too. There's nothing better than sharing your space with someone supportive.

And I think it's great that you got a dog. Please send a picture of it if you can, and if you have any questions, don't hesitate to ask. I know Connor would be happy to help.

Speaking of Connor, we got married a few days ago.

It was a small ceremony- just like I always wanted- and only our closest friends were there.

It was great to spend some time together because he's been traveling a lot, training other vets on how to work with the technology he invented.

I'm very proud of him, and it's wonderful to see him making such a big difference to so many animals and their families.

Meanwhile, I'm finally making a living from my painting. I've totally taken over for Gwendolyn, and I'm running my own workshops, too. It's been hard work getting it started, but the still life class for bachelorette parties has proved particularly popular in some of the surrounding areas.

Unfortunately, because of all the business craziness, we're postponing our honeymoon for a while, but to be honest, I don't mind. Every day feels like a honeymoon with him.

He is so loving and attentive, and I feel so blessed to have such a strong man in my life. I have no doubt that he is going to be a wonderful father.

Which is important because I'm pregnant!

So far, only Helly knows, but we're planning on telling our friends soon.

I'm a little nervous because I don't know the first thing about babies, but surely the hardest part is finding a village to help you raise them, and I think I've finally found that.

It feels good to belong somewhere- not just to fit in- but to really belong, and I wouldn't want to raise the baby anywhere else.

Just between us, it's a girl. I can't believe it. I know Connor especially wanted a girl, even though he would never have admitted it out loud, so I know he'll be my rock when she comes.

We haven't picked a name yet because I feel like I need to meet her first, but we've had lots of fun ruling some out.

It's strange how much my life looks like I always thought it would these days and how much it doesn't at the same time. Still, I'm happy, and I think of you often.

I know I say it a lot, but I really appreciate that you've respected my need for space and time. However, when the baby's born, it would mean a lot to me if you would come meet her.

I can't give you a specific date or anything yet, but I'll be in touch.

Look after yourself in the meantime.

Love and hugs,

Laney

Other books in the Soulmates Series